OLD OPEN

OLD OPEN

ALEX HIGLEY

TORTOISE BOOKS

CHICAGO, IL

FIRST EDITION, NOVEMBER, 2017

Published in the United States by Tortoise Books

www.tortoisebooks.com

ASIN: XXX
ISBN-10: 0-9986325-3-8
ISBN-13: 978-0-9986325-3-7

A version of the first chapter appears as the story "Rhymes with Feral" in the collection *Cardinal and Other Stories*

Cover painting by Slade Kaufman

Cover design by Andrew Wagner

Tortoise Books Logo Copyright ©2017 by Tortoise Books. Original artwork by Rachele O'Hare.

For my sister

PART I

It is two in the morning on my Friday, which is Tuesday, and in the house across the street, lights are getting flipped off and on in a disoriented march towards darkness. I'm watching the scene from my window with a ginger ale. Fifty-five and I still can't sleep. I've already had my allotment of three domestic light beers for the night and have switched to the other carbonated without regret. The home across the street belongs to, but is not occupied by, Terrell Presley. Standing in the middle of the street that separates our houses, in the rocky desert hills where we live, I asked him a while back one burning, ticking day if the light switches in his house were placed oddly, if there had been miswiring, because this stunted fluttering with the lights always happens with his renters, and he, not unkindly, ignored the question. The creasing around his eyes deepened and he half smiled beyond me, as if a person we both liked was arriving. I want to be able to elegantly ignore questions without malice or consequence. But I really was curious about the switches, all the lights blinking. I've never been in the house and can only guess at causation.

Terrell takes extravagant quarterly golf trips with men he's known since boyhood. Men he grew up with just outside of

Pittsburgh. Right now he's in Scotland. Last year was Brazil, at a resort where mostly undressed women offered kebabs mid-course. He told me cryptically: "I did not partake." Terrell has never been married, and in general, despite what these mildly salacious golf trip details might lead you to believe, is discreet.

I like Terrell because he is self-made and direct, even at his most opaque. He invented a surgical adhesive technology, sold it, and retired. He drives the same car he did pre-retirement, a pristine old Saab. He has always, until now, made a point to tell me a little about the person or people who will be renting, and reminds me to not hesitate to call the resort or him directly if there are any problems. I work from home, remotely doing IT consulting, and in all cases deal with his renters in a more concrete way than he ever does, even when I don't meet them. Past renters have included an ancient couple from Ames, Iowa; a retired military chaplain; Terrell's dim and gawking sister. He'd made sure to point out his sister was adopted. I've helped kill a snake, jump-started a car, and, by telephone, recommended restaurants, doctors, the most affordable liquor stores. I've been told my phone number is the only contact Terrell lists on the fridge. He knows I like to talk and don't mind questions from strangers.

Terrell doesn't seem interested to know my impressions of his renters. I usually open on his terms, asking, "Did the check clear?" But I wasn't able to do this with his sister, feeling it would be an overstep, so I'd had conspicuously little to say. From my window I'd seen her once, charging angrily in sweatpants towards her truck. I couldn't reconcile her seemingly plain yokel qualities with Terrell's daily crispness. So on his return, I only asked why she drove such an enormous truck, a Ford F-350. He told me he didn't know, but said, "Without the truck, would you have asked anything about her?" before heading back inside with his hands in his pockets. It occurred to me Terrell had bought his sister the truck. Maybe to give her some mystery. I have no proof.

Invariably, we have our talks in the middle of the cambered desert-worn street sloping between our two houses. The asphalt has been baked gray and is flecked by divots. We live north of Phoenix in Cave Creek, a place people travel to for their own golf vacations, which is the reason Terrell usually has no trouble filling the house in his absence. I've been told he could charge double his price. Our part of the desert is craggy and undulating. We have flat red peaks. Tan and pink bluffs, guajillo, Mexican Blue Palm, adobe houses tucked behind dog-leg driveways. I've found houses in Cave Creek to often be secretly opulent or secretly run-down. It's not exactly that all the houses look the same from the street, but instead that their flatness and positioning give away nothing. Landscaping is camouflage here. Locals take pride in the brutality of the summers, but I say any weather great masses of people over age ninety choose to be alive in, is weaker than advertised. Or over age fifty, for that matter. Nothing like the Midwestern crush and tumult of winter, the sickening cold. And here, if things do get too bad, San Diego is a five-hour drive, Flagstaff only two. As far as the renters that stay in his house, Terrell doesn't need the money, but something about his general practicality must prevent him from letting it sit empty when it could be generating profit.

I'm at the window watching his house, now steadily dark, considering what has changed between Terrell and me. I shift my weight standing, sciatica buzzing down through my ass into my deadened leg; daily, nightly, I'm crumbling. Sometimes more than others. He'd said Scotland, offered the information freely, and when I'd asked about renters, he'd told me there would be none. So who the fuck is over there?

o

I've slept late. It's nearly ten. I call Terrell's house, to see if the unregistered stranger will pick up—but the phone rings and rings. I walk into the kitchen to make breakfast. I put coffee on. I take out a non-stick skillet, spray it with olive oil, mix five eggs in a metal bowl, dump them in the skillet, now hot, and add a handful of shredded sharp cheddar cheese. I take out a can of black beans and microwave them in a Pyrex bowl. I take out tortillas from the fridge. I continue cooking the eggs as the coffeemaker sputters to completion. I have no idea how anyone makes scrambled eggs. I've been doing it this way for ten years now because I can't remember how my wife did it. My phone rings. The caller ID reads: TERRELL PRESLEY-HOME.

I say, "Yes, hello, this is Russ."

"You just called?" A woman's voice.

"Yes, I did. Terrell usually lets me know when he has a renter, so I was just calling to make sure everything is OK."

"If I'm not supposed to be here, how would calling the house help?"

"I don't know how to...are you supposed to be there?"

"Yeah. Terrell is supposed to be here too. I'm not renting. I'm a friend."

"It's pronounced 'tchr-ull.' Like feral." What kind of friend would mispronounce his name? He's a Terrell like Terrell Owens, not Terrell Davis.

"I've never said it out loud," the stranger says.

I don't know what to make of this. "Well, when does he get back from Scotland?"

The woman laughs. "I have no idea why he would have told you he was in Scotland. He's in Taos. He was supposed to be back yesterday before I arrived, but there was trouble with the plane."

I hang up with the woman and call Terrell. He answers on the first ring, and I ask if he knows there is a woman at his house. He says he knows, that everything is fine, and thank you, and that he should be back tomorrow. I can tell he's ready to hang up, but before he does, I ask, "Why doesn't she know how to pronounce your name?"

"I believe in the past she's always said 'Mr. Presley.' Been in rooms with me where that was the norm." And then he does hang up.

He didn't sound surprised or annoyed. He sounded like he always does, calm and already mentally occupied with other concerns. I put the phone down, spend a few minutes finishing the eggs, and my doorbell rings.

Standing at my front door is a thick-eyebrowed woman in workout clothes. Behind her, on the street she crossed to reach my home, heat is rising off the asphalt in blurring waves. She's wearing earbuds attached to a phone she has in an inside pocket of her open zip-up. Under the zip-up she is wearing a white sports bra. She's young, maybe thirty, and seems unaffected by the heat. Her dark hair is in a ponytail.

"I figured if I introduced myself, you'd see everything is OK. I'm Terrell's friend, Jordan."

I step aside so she can come into the house, say "Sure, sure," in sincere welcome, and we shake hands. Shaking hands with a beautiful woman usually makes me think of one of two scenarios: 1. If the handshake is strong, her father. 2. If the handshake is weak, her single working mother, and the apartment she'd had to herself, the thousands of hours of TV. I know this is fantasy, but, still, it remains. Jordan's was strong. Her loving father might have had no hands for all I know. No arms. The thought passes. To aid my unvoiced apology for the suspicions I earlier perpetrated on the phone, I ask Jordan if she wants any eggs, she says, "Sure, please," and I am more surprised by this than anything she has so far told me today. She is still wearing the headphones. The presence of another person in my kitchen makes me aware of its particulars: the size of the island suggesting a level of cooking I can't fulfill, the still-hanging decorative copper roosters my wife loved, the dated brightness and comfortable femininity. Jordan sits at the island as if she was a regular customer. Her attention is not diverted by any interest in scrutinizing my home: she seems already familiar, or, possibly closer to the truth, unimpressed.

"Do you always keep those in?" I ask, pointing at my own ears. I'm standing against the cabinets in the corner of the kitchen, intent on appearing as non-threatening as I am.

"You're the second person to say that to me today. Well, not quite. The guy at the grocery store asked me what I was listening to, and I lied to him. I told him, 'Richard and Linda Thompson,' thinking that would stop the conversation. I was wrong. The kid lit up. He went on about how he felt they 'got in their own way a lot,' but when they didn't they were 'really magic.' He cited 'I Want to See the Bright Lights Tonight' and a particular live version of 'A Heart Needs a Home' as evidence."

I make a face at Jordan. I haven't listened to or talked about Richard and Linda Thompson with anyone in twenty years, or longer. I shift on my feet because leaning against the counter is killing my back. By the way she was talking, even if she wasn't listening to Richard and Linda Thompson, she is making it clear she is familiar with their work. She seems dressed the wrong way to be saying the things she's saying, and too young, but this is a simple dumbass thought I try to get rid of. And I don't really know what the grocer meant. "What *were* you listening to?" I ask, getting her eggs situated on a tortilla I'd microwaved, scooping black beans over top.

"Nothing. I walk around with headphones in so people won't bother me, but it hasn't been working since I got here." She tells me she is from Toronto. She watches me construct her breakfast without comment, sarcastic or otherwise, which is touching, and she thanks me as I set the plate in front of her. She takes out her headphones, picks up the taco, and eats.

Her mouth full, I ask, "Why is Terrell in Taos?"

"A convention," Jordan says, covering her mouth with her hand. "But I was unaware that you were unaware. Earlier, I mean."

"Of what?" I ask, wanting her to say more.

"Of who Terrell is," she says. "Of what he does." She types something into her phone and holds it out to me.

Before I look, I say, "Does he know that you are going to tell me whatever you're going to tell me?"

"He knows you know he's in Taos," Jordan says, shrugging. "I called him before I came over. And he said he *was* in Scotland for a few days, before Taos. He told me that."

Terrell's been gone five days. To and from Scotland is a full day of flying. It's *possible* he was in Scotland before returning to the States, to Taos. But why?

I put on my cheaters and take the phone from Jordan. On the phone is a Wikipedia entry for "Phoenix Lights." I look at Jordan. She is again mid-bite. The entry reads:

> *The Phoenix Lights (also identified as "Lights over Phoenix") was a UFO sighting which occurred in Phoenix, Arizona, and Sonora, Mexico on Thursday, March 13, 1997. Lights of varying descriptions were reported by thousands of people between 19:30 and 22:30 MST, in a space of about 300 miles (480 km), from the Nevada line, through Phoenix, to the edge of Tucson. There were allegedly two distinct events involved in the incident: a triangular formation of lights seen to pass over the state, and a series of stationary lights seen in the Phoenix area. The United States Air Force later identified the second group of lights as flares dropped by A-10 Warthog aircraft that were on training exercises at the Barry Goldwater Range in southwest Arizona.*

I'm not following. I hold out the phone for Jordan, who is looking through my cupboards for a mug. When I point to the right spot, she gets one and pours herself coffee. I ask her what the deal is, and she says, "Keep reading."

I audibly huff, and she smiles and drinks her coffee. I've succeeded in being non-threatening, dad-like. I scroll past sections detailing the timeline of the events, the arrival of the first and second set of lights in Prescott, Dewey, and Phoenix. Scroll past a heading of "First Sighting in Phoenix," and "Reappearance in 2007," and "Reappearance in 2008." I scroll until I reach a section of the entry titled "Photographic Evidence." Details of the photographic evidence of the first event yield nothing of interest; I go to the second event, and jackpot:

During the Phoenix event, numerous still photographs and videotapes were made, distinctly showing a series of lights appearing at a regular interval, remaining illuminated for several moments and then going out. Terrell Presley, of Cave Creek, captured the most often reproduced of these images. Presley's photographs were all taken from the upper level of a Phoenix parking garage near Phoenix Sky Harbor International Airport. These images have been repeatedly aired by documentary television channels such as the Discovery Channel and the History Channel as part of their UFO documentary programming. [...] The most frequently reproduced sequence shows what appears to be an arc of lights appearing one by one, then going out in the same fashion. UFO advocates claim that these images show that the lights were some form of "running light" or other aircraft illumination along the leading edge of a large craft — estimated to be as large as a mile (1.6 km) in diameter — hovering over the city of Phoenix. Thousands of witnesses throughout Arizona also reported a silent, mile-wide V or

boomerang-shaped craft with varying numbers of huge
orbs. A significant number of witnesses reported that
the craft was silently gliding directly overhead at low
altitude.

"He's not golfing," I say.

"He golfs. He just also gives talks. He was giving a talk in
Taos. That's probably what he was doing in Scotland. There
are UFO conventions all over the world. That's where I met
Mr. Presley. At a talk he gave in Toronto a year ago."

A year ago. I'm trying to remember where Terrell told me
he'd gone, but I can't remember. He could've said Canada.

The Phoenix Lights would have happened three months after
my wife and I moved to Arizona from Chicago. 1997. Eighteen
years ago. I was thirty-seven and she was thirty-nine, no kids,
no dog. I was still looking for a new job. I didn't know it at
the time, but it would be another two anxious months of
unemployment. She was working all sorts of shifts at the
hospital, crazy hours, hours she didn't need to work, to prove
to her staff she was one of them, and had arrived to stay. They
learned quickly the kind of woman she was. I still get cards
from these women on her birthday, on my birthday, on days
less readily marked. Undoubtedly she was working the night
these alien lights hung in the sky, the night Terrell was on
the top level of a parking garage taking pictures. Why was he
up there? Was he some kind of photographer? Is the answer
he was up there because he had the time? I don't know if he'd
sold his adhesive patent by then or not. I don't know what his

nights were filled with. Certain types of people don't see UFOs would be my guess: people who are paycheck-to-paycheck, people with three kids, sick people, people with tangible worries and jobs. But this could be wrong. Maybe witnesses to these events span demographics, maybe because they actually happen.

We had an apartment on the fourth floor, and on her days off we'd sit in shorts on our little deck and watch the sunset, ask each other, "Would you move back to Chicago if you could?" And we'd both say, "No, I wouldn't. I like it here." Neither of us believed the other completely. We'd left all our friends and moved to a new state where the people were different, more private, and we'd found we were more unwilling to make new friends than we realized. We liked people, both of us; we liked people we didn't know, we liked waiters and pharmacists and kids on airplanes. I mean, we hated all these people too, but I'm just saying we were not wary of everyone unknown to us. We were open, just less open than we'd realized before we'd moved, but we became happier clinging to each other, married in a way we never knew we could be.

I vaguely remember reading about the Phoenix Lights in the paper. Front page news. But I didn't care about the event. Not in the slightest. I felt this way, feel this way, because of course there are aliens. Even if the lights aren't extraterrestrial, if the reality is that the lights were some military happening, of course there is still something out there. The specifics aren't important to me until the manifestation of alien life appearing on our planet moves past this speculative era. The difference for me is that life is enough. Normal routine nothing is enough. I'm interested in maps and pop music and recycling. Slow movies and the rainforest. Ocean fish that pulse glowing at pitch-black depths. And baseball. Tintypes of my forebears. Helmets from the Han dynasty or pre-merger football. The house across the street. My thinking is, aren't we enough? Huddling together in hotel ballrooms and convention centers to affirm the actuality of an event past seems a waste. There's actuality happening right now. In abundance. But I could be missing the point.

Terrell and I didn't speak until after my wife died. We'd wave to him as we were building this house in Cave Creek, and he'd wave back, but we didn't engage in any conversations in the middle of the street or elsewhere. My wife said at the time that Terrell looked like William Faulkner, then she said Howard Hughes, or a short actor playing Howard Hughes in a community theater production.

"A production of what?" I remember asking.

"*Melvin and Howard*," she said, to please me. She knew that the idea of the Demme movie done onstage would make me grin. We'd seen *All the President's Men* at a ten-year anniversary release in '86, on our first date in Rogers Park near the Loyola campus at a theater long since gone, and Robards had remained something like our patron saint ever since. We'd met at Loyola, in an English class, a minor for both of us. I'd said this to Terrell early on, told him my wife had thought he looked like Faulkner, and he'd squinted his small eyes and said he'd never been told that. I think he started telling me about his renters because during that first talk after we were caught checking the mail at the same time, he needed something to say to the widower. To me.

Jordan is washing her own plate and mug, and I'm letting her do so without protest. She finishes, makes eye contact with me, and then looks away, meaning she is going to be heading out. I walk her to the door and she steps outside, turning to me and saying, "When Terrell gets back you should come over for drinks, the three of us." Whatever she knows about Terrell is very different than what I know of him, so although I say in my head, "That will never happen," maybe it will. It occurs to me to say, "Today is my Friday, so tomorrow could still work," but then I'd have to explain that for the past several years, since beginning remote consulting, I've reinstated the work schedule of my youth in retail. Friday to Tuesday. It made sense to return to the schedule I knew before married life, to shopping in empty grocery stores midweek. For my life to lack any family rhythm. I say, "Sure, you bet," about potentially drinking together and give her an earnest thumbs-up before she begins back across the street. She takes four steps—I know because I'm watching her walk away too closely, I'm human—before I say: "Jordan."

She stops and faces me.

"What's the big fucking secret?" I ask. "Why wouldn't Terrell just tell me where he was going? What he was doing?"

"Maybe he was afraid things would change," she says. "Or maybe he thought you already knew."

And I have to remind myself she doesn't know the state of our understanding of one another, how brief and situational our connections are. We speak in the middle of the street about people who will be staying at Terrell's house a handful of times a year. I relay information about past renters. We wave. I do not ask Terrell personal questions; I respect the boundaries he maintains through his silence on topics he wishes to avoid. I try to make him laugh, and occasionally get a wry smile, which is just as satisfying. It's possible that Jordan is right about Terrell being against a change in our situation. I can see how if Terrell likes being perceived as a person who keeps up with boyhood pals and takes them golfing around the world (in my previous understanding it was Terrell who paid for dinners and drinks and possibly even hotel rooms for these men) he would not want my perception dashed. Maybe he was able to see himself in the way I saw him because of our talks. Maybe he believes I know of his UFO talks and the golf and can hold those two facts in my head at once without ever speaking of the former. Maybe his understanding was that other people in town had told me of his Phoenix Lights fame and the reason our arrangement worked was because I chose to not ask him of it. Because what was there to say? What is there to say? You believe or you don't, regardless of content. Maybe he knew me to be a believer, in general, and so any talk of inner self-definition and purpose was beside the point. The point was he'd found, in part, an equal. Maybe he wants me to be able to live inside my own created worlds, as I have done for him. I won't be able to ask these questions of Terrell, not in a way that would give me the answers I want to know. And should I ask, I imagine he would raise his eyes to the horizon.

I've heard it said colloquially that the ability to communicate is unlimited if a certain openness is allowed by both parties; I believe this to be far from the truth. The amount of self-knowledge pre-supposed in a word like "openness" is vast. Our neighborly pattern feels irreparably altered.

o

Terrell's back. After hearing his garage door motor, I perform my halting stagger to the window to see him and Jordan pull away in the Saab. This happens a few times, and I get no invite for drinks.

She leaves sometime after I've lost track of their comings and goings because an accounting program I helped design for an after-market golf cart accessory manufacturer in the Valley has gone awry. I have to videoconference with the same in-house tech guy for three days straight, giving him the language to calm his three bosses and an understanding of how to fix the books. I tell him at one point, when he is losing all patience with the tasks he sees stacked waiting in the days ahead, that we are talking about golf cart canopies and GPS systems to determine shot lengths for a leisure sport. This is not life-or-death. He is not calmed. He tells me, "It is my job to be worried." I try and let his words stand for him by not responding, in order for him to be able to hear what he's said and re-examine its content. But I don't think this happens. I'm certain it doesn't.

②

Anticipating change following Jordan's visit, I've placed a sticky note next to my front window to track Terrell. The plan is to mark each time I see him check the mail or drive off somewhere. I have a feeling I've crossed a boundary, that Terrell will be less forthcoming—even more secretive in his movements than he has been previously. Although I didn't understand he was being particularly secretive before. He was private. If I wanted to reach him, I could. I hadn't meant to reorganize the way in which we were neighbors. I only wanted to know who was across the street. And now that I've found out, I want to know who's been *living* across the street for all these years. Anyway, the sticky is blank: a bright square mocking my watch. There has been no sign of life at Terrell's in four days until now. A boxy black van purrs up his drive.

The van settles high on Terrell's driveway like a guest. Two women spill out the front seats and open the back, grab vacuum, broom, cleaning supplies. They make a small pile of their tools near Terrell's front door and let themselves in. I don't know how this access was arranged. Neither woman stooped to reach under a mat. A key was dropped off? Where? At one of the cleaning lady's houses? How many house-cleaning operations have brick-and-mortar locations?

The van is the thing, right? But lots of house cleaners don't have vans. I remember seeing many people in the cleaning business traveling in late-eighties Honda Accords, blue, with the old sunrise California plates, not vans.

Arrangements have been made with outside entities for upkeep. This is new; in the past Terrell did his own post-visitor cleaning. Terrell is gone, his house seems empty, and his departure feels long-term. "Permanent" seems ridiculous. Who would move because their neighbor now knows the truth about their UFO trips? I've caused nothing. But now that I've laid out the thought before me, it seems likely Terrell will move. Maybe some other aspect of his life has escalated? Demanded his attention? It might have nothing to do with me.

I have investigations in my days. In my working days and days off. It's because I don't have a wife anymore, have never had dependents or a dog, work from home (less and less) and am generally, increasingly, unsure. I become fixated on a subject, a person, an image, and pursue; there is no one in my life to check me.

Maybe you're thinking: an aching fifty-five-year-old man, a widower, obsessive, computer literate—I get it, we're talking porn. But we're not. Maybe you're thinking that because you live alone. Maybe you're thinking that because you're married yourself and have thought, idly, walking through a crowded sunny outlet mall or at the gym: If my wife died, would the world allow me to have sex with that redhead in the striped shirt and cat-eye sunglasses? Or the smiling freckled blonde that lived on the seventh floor in the dorms back in college? Someone like her? And you're thinking porn because from what you already know of me, standing at the window with a ginger ale, actual sex seems like a stretch. There's some of that in my life, sure, but it's quick. I try to get as many daily tasks completed as I can in the shower. Teeth, dread, shave, etc. But as far as the fantasy fuck thinking— well, wait until your wife dies. That kind of thinking becomes less stirring. Present, but less stirring.

You weren't thinking porn at all, were you? You're surprised I even used the word.

Regardless, by "investigation" I mean something more along the lines of making sure I understand basic concepts and relationships that already are functioning in my life. I was on the phone with a client in Sun City recently, and he expressed jealousy that I was able to work from home. This is a mostly retired man who had spent his working life in midtown Manhattan. Retired in the sense that he does not work daily, has no boss, but has ceded his second business life as a franchisee owner of a southwestern hamburger restaurant chain to his son and now takes calls he does not trust his son to handle properly himself. His jealousy was retrospective. He said some form of: don't know if I could do it, would be nice to be home, takes discipline. Then he added, and I remember this part verbatim, "You're doing honest work."

He was an old friendly man giving me a worn friendly line, but the phrase stayed with me for the rest of the night. I searched the phrase online. I read through quotations allegedly related to "honest work" compiled by *Forbes* in order to form what resembled an online article on the topic. Part of the introduction to the list:

> *Here are 70 insightful, often inspiring quotations about the glory of honest work and the folly of government policies that promote idleness.*

But most of the quotations, at least the ones that resonated, didn't seem to be related to "honest work" at all. The quotations were focused on the value of money, on having money, or on the value of "hard" work. The connection between "hard" and "honest" is not clear to me, probably because there is no connection. Quote #69:

> *"Work keeps at bay three great evils: boredom, vice and need."*
>
> *Voltaire, Candide (1759)*

But can't dishonest work keep away boredom, vice, and need? Especially if the person working is unaware that his or her work is dishonest? Because what is honest work? And what if the value of preventing "three great evils" from entering one's life is greater than the importance of the method of their prevention? In other words, what if the method of their prevention is dishonest work? Quote #70:

> *"Nothing ever comes to one, that is worth having, except as a result of hard work."*
>
> *Booker T. Washington, Up From Slavery (1901)*

Is hard work hard because it is constant? Is hard work difficult work? Or is hard work complicated work? Many jobs that are uncomplicated are difficult. Shoveling rocks is difficult work but is uncomplicated. Is uncomplicated work honest work? Not necessarily. A rock-shoveling business could charge triple their competitors for the same job. But is this dishonest? What if the service is advertised as luxury rock shoveling? What prevents the client from going elsewhere with their business? Is pricing even related to the morality of work?

And so, like this, nightly, I am in knots. I am not faulting the compiler of these quotations, nor the publication that allowed them grouped, not at all. I just have this great wish that at the top of articles, in place of the banner ads attempting to sell me the game-worn Chicago Bears TK Suspension helmets that so easily hypnotize me on eBay, there was, in red, writ large: INCOMPLETE/PROVISIONAL/AN ATTEMPT. And maybe there is, inherently. I need to remind myself of that.

The quote that struck me most of the seventy and returns me now to Terrell, to his time and how he spent it, spends it, to his current unannounced departure:

> *"Without money, there's no leisure, without leisure no thought, without thought no progress."*
>
> *Frederick Douglass, Speech in St. Michaels, Maryland (1877)*

Terrell has the time to travel around the country, the world, and give talks on UFOs. He had the time to take photographs of the Phoenix Lights. He has the time to think about the lights, spread his photographs, meet others like himself, and continue to progress within this interest of his, this experience. I may not be interested in UFOs, but I am interested in my world, especially the people and happenings in my daily life. And, like Terrell, I have time.

I don't *have* to work anymore, at least not doggedly so. I'm fifty-five. The house is nearly paid off. I have some money saved. I don't have enough money to retire, not if I live another thirty years. Not if I live another fifteen. Not if I want to start traveling. Not if I am unwilling to sell this house. But I do have enough money to take a couple weeks off and attempt to figure out why Terrell was unable to tell me who he is. To try to understand some of why he is able to give talks, speak passionately (I'm assuming passion) to strangers about UFOs, bed young Canadian women, and yet give me no hint.

I understand the core of Terrell's inability to tell me who he is, apart from his specific motive. I don't mind questions from strangers. I invite them. I know the appeal of a stranger and that her most entertaining trait is her brevity. Her contextlessness, her brief, partial, reality. The loss of a stranger's company is expected, welcomed, and, at best, in place of her company, dreamy tendrilled speculation moves in. A stranger cannot be known, by definition, but certainly can be understood. I have the desire to be understood, and hate the idea of being known. I want to communicate, speak clearly, but don't feel the need to broadcast where I was born, my beer preference, college degrees, childhood sadnesses, my wife's name, the last movie that made me cry—scratch that, the last movie I finished watching. Some of this leaks out, and I'm not hiding, but my preference is to be unknown. Understood but unknown. Terrell might be the same. And in some ways, I know he is.

"Known" is burdened with history, with memories, deals in and becomes a shorthand with an ignorance of the person present. And so I try to avoid being known to most people. Not all, but most. I'm reminded of a line from a Joy Williams novel that's always stayed with me, a favorite book of my wife's: "Liberty guessed that Willie enjoyed a simple deceit more than just about anything in the world." That's how I feel. Lying to a stranger, telling him I too am from Nebraska, as it reads on his sweatshirt, or telling another man that we must have something in common because when I lived in Tampa I drove an MG in that exact shade of mallard green, makes me feel wonderful. It's because I know then that the stranger is starting at a deficit in truly knowing who I am, but, if I am lucky, also might feel close to me. My wife kept this in check, would stop me mid-sentence with clerks, "He's lying. Don't listen." But, I don't have anyone to check me anymore. Maybe I don't mind questions from strangers because I don't feel the need to tell the truth.

Honest work is understandable work. I think that's it.

As I've already posited, it's possible that Terrell thought I knew about him and the Lights and that I was choosing not to ask him of it. It's possible that the reason Terrell tolerated me at all was because he believed I was exercising this restraint. If this is true, that he thought I knew and chose to say nothing, he must have thought me incredibly strange to press him on other lesser topics like his opinion of modern Terry Bradshaw, and that I ultimately accepted his non-responses, his looks to the distance, and yet never pressed him on that which made him famous. He must have thought me remarkable.

o

I walk into my backyard. The sun is full up, late morning, and I am wearing shorts that are high above my knee. I can feel heat at my ankles, on the tops of my feet, on my bald spot. I'm gingerly rotating in place to try and unlock my back. Sciatica down my left cheek and numb leg. I scruff the little hair I do have as if I've just gotten my hair cut. The idea of joying in a haircut makes me boyish and hopeful, despite my posture. My backyard gently slopes downward. A nice broad slant of desert rectangle hemmed in by a low pink wall. The joke I have in my head, or rather, the name I've given my backyard that makes more sense if presented as a joke, is: family burial plot, or, F.B.P. The name appears in my days when I walk outside and greet my borrowed land, say, "Another day, Effbeepee." I am playing the role of widower by naming my ragged backyard, and for some reason this role-playing is life affirming. No one is buried here, but a family of four or five would be more than comfortable. A real motherfucker to dig out though. I squint and hold it, reveling in the heat of the day.

Beyond F.B.P., I have a view of Black Mountain and its wide set of peaks. The range I have in my sight, the range that surrounds me, is the McDowell, inhospitable and orange in the morning, glow-red at sunsets, brown-burred in the day. These mountains kill hikers regularly. I have neighbors but not up close. The houses around me, and my own, look strewn, as if our homes were set down in this hilly desert but then twisted in their moorings by a storm or several. I close my eyes and try to think of people in town that I want to ask about Terrell. I'd like to know what my wife would say of what has occurred between our two houses. She'd nail it, be sure. Say something like, "It's all in your head. Let's eat." Saying I am trying to think of people to ask about Terrell is disingenuous. I am thinking about *how* to ask two specific people, Barnes and his wife Lucia, about Terrell. Barnes and Lucia Umber, owners of Umber's. Umber's is a strip mall breakfast restaurant in Phoenix near the hospital where my wife worked when she was alive. The vinyl seating at Umber's is aquamarine and pink, the plates are oval shaped, there are TVs squawking news. The Umbers live nearby, here in Cave Creek, and I can walk to their home in fifteen minutes. Walking here is a signifier of distress. So it might be the most honest mode of travel for me. Before I go after Terrell, find out where he has gone, track him down, and talk to him like some cub journalist with something to prove, I feel the need to test my hypotheses locally.

③

I call and get Barnes, and he says, "Come." He pauses. "Come for dinner." I tell him I'll be there at seven if that works. I'll get the first of the sunset this way. He lets out a long whistle and hangs up, which lets me know Lucia was in the room with him while he was on the phone. Barnes is a lovable show-off who likes nothing more than achieving an eye-roll from his wife. Their marriage is full of wonderfully strange boundaries and frankness, some of which I can relate to, but most of which is sweetly bizarre to witness, that is, if you are able to believe it. The Umbers were the couple we hung out with as a couple. A generation older than us in all ways.

o

Lucia opens the door, "Why are you sweating so hard? You didn't walk, did you? You're in trouble?" I feel as if she is addressing Lassie as I stand soaked. I resist barking. She's a frazzled tall woman who seems to have been frayed by raising wild boys, which is what happened. Both her sons are in their mid-forties and have professions related to dirt bikes. Mirror walls and art fill Lucia and Barnes' home. All the art has acquisition dates beginning and ending in the final half of the 1980s. That Duran Duran record with the woman's face on it seems to be the dowsing object the Umbers used to choose pieces for their home.

At home, their cooking stands in opposition to what is regularly served at Umber's. Tonight, dinner is a spinach salad, tossed with avocado, baked tempeh that has been allowed to cool slightly, and lemon squeezed overtop. With the salad we will be drinking frozen mango margaritas. My allotment increases to unlimited when with others. This was not always the case. Frozen mangos, ice, tequila, agave nectar. I have had this exact meal at the Umbers' home before. I don't know if their comfort in repetition has to do with age, or because they are a certain type of restaurant people, but I say "comfort" because they never apologize for serving the same meal to me. Not that they should; they should serve whatever they want in their home. But I love that they are comfortable enough to not ask me what I'd like.

Barnes is intently making up the salads in the kitchen, elbows out, and says only "Russ" in greeting. Lucia nods at me to follow her out of the white kitchen and onto the back patio. Their sliding glass door works luxuriously well. An oiled brushy sound. I grab the door's handle and slide the door back and forth a few times. Lucia claps into the gloaming, towards the far corners of her backyard, the golf corner and the cacti corner, I'm guessing to spurn any wildlife.

We have our margaritas in chilled glass beer steins with large handles. We sit at an outdoor glass table in cushioned, springy chairs capable of being leaned back in. We settle in to the heat.

Lucia's shoulder-length frizzled gray hair appears shocked by humidity, but is not, because there is none tonight. You might expect that she is a potter, a painter, a woman eagerly cataloging desert flora—but she is none of those things. She's a businesswoman, and a good one at that. If you combined all my mental strength and real world effort with that of Barnes, we could not hold a candle to what this woman is capable of, and daily doing. She is general manager, front of house, her husband's lodestar.

And one day a week she cooks at the restaurant. Thursday, or as it has become known to regulars, "Hippie Thursday." I said the Umbers' cooking at home stands apart from what is served at the restaurant, but this isn't true on Thursdays, when the two fares are in distant unison. Thursdays at the restaurant, the menu is limited, avocados featuring largely. The plates come out prettier, more fussed over, and sugar is removed from the restaurant in its most egregious forms. Ketchup, coffee sweeteners on the table, jellies, jams, are all lined up neatly in a blank corner of the kitchen waiting for their reintroduction on Friday morning.

I've asked Lucia, why not convert the restaurant's menu completely? And she told me it wouldn't be fair to the boomers. To the Sallys, Ricks, Burts, Nancys, Esthers. "When they die off, it's fair," she'd said, and Barnes added, seeing the rare gap in his wife's thinking, "When we die off, sweetie. When we die off."

The last of the sun is holding on the horizon: the condensed day melting down. It's still over ninety degrees outside, but it's nice to sit with a view of the low shady mountains. Their backyard has a centrally located water feature, water spilling from flat tan rocks into a pool I could have leaped over if I was younger and didn't have a numb left leg. The sound of the water stands in for music. Though they're only around ten years older than me, listening to a fountain seems like the preference of ancients. There's a putting green in the far-right corner of the yard, which is bordered by a pink brick wall identical to the one in my own backyard. Lucia takes a long slug of her margarita, the orange slush glacially shifting down the glass, and closes her eyes. I look over again and she's darting her tongue in and out of her mouth, eyes still closed, lizard-style. I try doing the same but imagine I look instead like a weary dog. But it's not an impression I can hold—dogs don't have words to reveal their small minds, as we do. I would like to be reduced, without worrying anyone, to an old dog's regal honest grunting.

Barnes brings the first salad out to Lucia, and I start to stand to go help him with the rest, but he clasps me on the shoulder and commands, "Stay." This demonstrative hosting is totally unnecessary and hasn't really been present on prior nights with the Umbers. Barnes wants prep and cleanup to be his overt burden.

Barnes is clear-blue-eyed, with uniform white bristles of hair all over his face and head. I've heard him say, many times, "One setting on my buzzer. Easy." I liked him the moment I met him because I knew the shorthand he was providing for who he was, and I sensed it to be genuine. In Chicago I knew a cheerful crooked landlord with the same bearing—and on the street in Rogers Park, Roscoe Village, Uptown, I passed fifteen Barnes' daily. He's a type, by choice. But if you knew him you'd be glad he's the sort of man he is.

"Work?" Lucia asks. A predatory bird silhouette passes evenly overhead. She inhales sharply through her nose, unrelated to the bird, and I chortle at the intensity of her breathing. This woman, and she's always been like this, seems as if she is discovering her body and its minute abilities for the first time. If my wife were here and able to read my thoughts, scratch that, if my wife was here, she'd add, "And she's a self-hating hypochondriac." She'd add this thought, tell me this thought, by a slight tuck of her lips, raise of the chin, in my direction.

"I'm taking some time off," I say about work. I try to inhale as Lucia just has, but can't achieve the sharp near whistle. Instead I sound like a man warding off tears.

"Oh?" Lucia says.

"A few weeks. I let my clients know today, referred them to a guy I worked with years ago in case they need help in my absence. My list is shrinking. He could use the work. Kids. Champagne taste, beer budget kind of guy. But nice." I hate the way I'm talking about this man. I look over and see Lucia nodding, listening. I say, "I hate the way I'm talking about this guy. He was the only person I could think of with the time and ability to potentially take on some extra work that I was still in contact with. His kids have nothing to do with anything—"

Lucia sets down her margarita on the scalloped glass table in front of us and puts up both hands towards me, palms out, meaning, stop. I stop. I hear the gurgle of their rubbly water fountain. The soft thrumming punch of insects. She says, "I don't care, I don't care. Say whatever you want. The point is you're here with us and we are glad you are. We can talk about flashlights. We can talk about Carson Palmer. Jake Plummer. We can talk shit about this guy you worked with. Don't fucking care."

I tell Lucia "OK, OK," and almost expect her to scruff me behind the ear like a puppy. That's how intense her grin is. Barnes comes out with the last two salads, hands one to me, and sits down with his own and begins eating. We all eat loudly, forks chiming, and gulp our margaritas. The salad bowls are enormous and change how I eat completely. I'm not used to having to take such a steep approach into a bowl, and as a result I'm really paying attention to the food. I covet this heavy bowl.

"He's taking off work," Lucia says.

"What for?" asks Barnes.

"I want to go see if I can track down Terrell Presley."

"Terrell across the street Terrell?" says Lucia.

"Why's that take a month?" Barnes asks.

"I don't know where he is at the moment. Or where he's going to be."

Barnes sits up from his hunched position over his bowl and settles back into his seat. He is giving me a look that projects how glad he is to not live alone. Lucia says, "Hold up," and walks into the house. She comes back out onto the patio holding the blender full of margaritas. She pours us all more. "OK, so what's happening?" she asks. "Be clear."

I cough in a way that sounds practiced, because it *was* practiced on my walk over. "Do you guys know about Terrell and the Phoenix Lights? How he took those pictures we've all seen? The ones the paper ran—"

Barnes says, "The triangle, sure."

Lucia adds, "We saw same as him. Wedge of lights."

"From here?"

"Right here," Lucia says. She traces a triangle in the sky above her with an index finger.

"You've never told me that."

"Aliens don't pay my rent," Lucia says, "Aliens ain't on my mind."

I consider not saying anything further. Speaking out loud—in detail—what has driven me to preemptively take time off work is embarrassing. Barnes says something to Lucia about where their own pictures of the Phoenix Lights are, and, Lucia seems to remember that Terrell purchased their photographs of the event from them. That he went door-to-door asking. That he offered cash. They are talking quietly to one another about this; I can hear pieces, and they know I can, but the talk is not inclusive. I'm watching as night sky emerges. If there were constellations to look at, if it were dark enough, I wouldn't know their names. I watch the sky dumbly but not without interest. I feel that what they can jointly remember about their pictures will determine whether or not they will raise their voices, repeat what they have just said to each other, and bring me back in to the fold.

I've drifted; I watch a brown lizard scurry between my feet towards the sculpted rock water feature. The gurgle calls him. Barnes and Lucia have stopped talking. I apologize for no reason.

I say, "I didn't know any of that about Terrell until recently. We talked occasionally and I helped out with his renters, but I didn't know he was giving talks—"

"Talks, sure. We went. We went in 2000. Great alien year," Barnes says. "I mean I'm sure it's evolved by now, the talk, new information, incorporation of new technology. But we've heard the basic Phoenix Lights talk, yes. Very inspiring. When he bought our pictures, he also asked for snapshots. Of Lucia and me. That was in the talk too."

I don't know what to make of this information. I push my margarita away from me on the table. "Do you think that Terrell thought *I* knew he was the Phoenix Lights guy?"

Lucia is smiling. She's taking her time. "This is a little like asking if your neighbor Charles Barkley believed you knew he played basketball. Barkley wouldn't have thought about what you knew or didn't know."

"Or neighbor Charles Manson murdered," Barnes added, rushing his words.

"The Phoenix Lights and Terrell, that's who he is," Lucia said.

I feel sick to my stomach. What else am I not seeing? When Lucia and Barnes went through some trouble (Lucia slept with a server she'd hired, a beautiful fat woman from New Mexico with long fake nails) they announced it to my wife and me during a raucous happy hour. "Out with it," Lucia said at the time, goading herself to confess, which she then did. These are not people that keep in information. Following her infidelity came the rededication to cooking, the elimination of most processed foods from their home (Barnes demanded 'Dr. Pepper stays'), the introduction of "Hippie Thursdays." What I'm saying is that if Lucia thought I didn't know about Terrell, I would have been told. Her understanding, Barnes' understanding (which is the trickle down of Lucia's understanding), was that I knew and did not care. I see now, with certainty, this was also Terrell's understanding. And why on Earth would they think anything else? I see now I have mistaken my cause for wanting to speak to Terrell, my problem, as needing scaffolding outside of myself. And really, I don't care anymore to speak to him. I want to be spoken to—to hear his talk. Understand who he is more clearly. I thought I needed justification for what I was planning to do. A reason. But I don't. What my problem needs is a city to travel to, a car to transport it, possibly a woman, my problem needs a meeting with its source, it needs an adventure, needs to get out of the goddamn heat.

Here's what I *do* know about Terrell, apart from aliens. All this from over a decade of brief outdoor chats. Born and raised in Pittsburgh, college at Penn for undergrad, stayed for an M.S.E. in Chemical and Biomolecular Engineering. I know he's proud of being from Pittsburgh. And I suspect he is funnier than he is allowing me to know. He is more comfortable projecting many of the clichéd trappings of wealth (large exception being his old Saab—although this too is cliché, worn khakis and a worn car belying lazy old money, early lacrosse hopes), displaying these invented trappings— like his slightly affected taciturn nature, and his golf vacations—instead of broadcasting who he really is. Actually, scratch that—he enjoys narrowcasting the clichéd trappings of wealth to his neighbor across the street, but I don't know why. And yet, he seems to be entertained by this neighbor, by me, to some extent. To some extent, he trusts me. He lists, listed, my phone number for his guests. He gave me information about when he would be gone. He gave me genuine partial truths. It's complicated between us. Thing is, I don't know if he knows this. His interactions with everyone might be equally as complicated, but unrecognized. I know Terrell is smarter than I am.

o

Most of the lights in my house are on. I'm in my living room flat on my back on the carpet. My sciatica is calm if I'm on my back, feet up on the coffee table. From the floor I can see my wife's knitting lamp at the far end of our pale orange couch, our chipped coffee table with unread copies of *The New Yorker* piled on top, my White Sox cap. Our bookshelves in the living room are full of my wife's books. All alphabetized, except a privileged few: *So Long, See You Tomorrow*, her Elizabeth Bishop, her William Stafford, etc. Her books have become my books. Her favorite lines, oft repeated, have become my own to keep close. But her books don't make her. And knowing the pages she knew does not give me her mind. I have no guilt about the unread magazines. I check the fiction and the long profile and set the magazine on the coffee table with the rest. Sometimes I will read an issue whole, but this is rare. Eventually I cull the stack based on covers. My house is cold and I feel safe within its machinations and hums. The clattering dump of the icemaker. The digital river sound of the air conditioning. The movie I have on in the background for some company. *An Autumn Afternoon*. The stillness and swelling transitions, the right angles, offices, homes, and willful daughters. I'm still a little drunk from the Umbers', the kind of drunk that wants to stay drunk. Unlimited allotment extends past social gatherings; they are infrequent. I have gin in the freezer, but no beer at present. I would love a beer. Love to be served a beer—to be young and be served a beer early in the night somewhere on the coast, on the East Coast, a mid-Atlantic wooden ramshackle bar on the beach, most of the crowd down near the shore, and I'm waiting for someone to arrive. I want music on. An engine roars outside.

Headlights. Another car at Terrell's and this time it's one I recognize. The Ford F-350 belonging to Terrell's younger sister. It's been close to a year since she last showed. She lives in Tennessee, in Knoxville, if what I was once told is still true, and thinking about the terror she must have caused en route—lazing into the center line, ferociously snapping at gas station attendants, sending back eggs for being scrambled "too hard," jolts me awake, afraid as I walk-limp out my front door to catch her.

I've never met this woman. I've seen her from afar, seen the truck back when she was housesitting. My impression of her is formed mainly by the way she blitzed to and from her vehicle, by the truck itself, and by the fact that during her last stay she twice called my phone number by mistake. First, thinking I was a man named Jerry, and then days later rushing headlong into ordering a pizza with red onions and "white-meat" chicken. (I told her, "We're out of red onion," and she said, "Guess it's fucking Chinese again," before hanging up.) In our brief conversations, Terrell hadn't seemed particularly impressed by how she'd turned out; I had the sense that her truck was her most notable quality.

I slowly huff up Terrell's drive in the dark with a sharp pain in my ass cheek and a stiffening back. I would not be so bold if I thought Terrell was here or I was sober. His sister is leaning into her truck, in jeans, with her back to me on

Terrell's driveway. I sexualize her without meaning to, a woman I'm predisposed not to like, dangerous territory, but from behind she *is* striking. I think, stop, and it's done. That trucks are often paired with guns in our part of the world, and hers, occurs to me. I say, "Excuse me?" She straightens.

"Excuse you?" Terrell's sister says. She's standing on the driver's side facing me and I can't see her left hand, it's somewhere in the truck. She looks completely unafraid, isn't wearing any makeup, and is more alert, more intelligent in the face than I remember. Looks younger than I expected. She is wearing a Creamsicle© orange Tennessee Vols jersey, cut off short to reveal her belly in the style of a fullback from three decades ago. She doesn't have any fat on her, which is discomfiting because she is possibly forty, and the phrase "she doesn't have any fat on her" sounds like farm talk, and because my next thought becomes, returns, am I attracted to this woman? I answer myself unintentionally aloud, a firm "No."

"You mean, 'Yes.' You're staring," she says.

"Sorry. I saw—heard your truck and wanted to run over and ask where Terrell is. I wanted to make sure he's OK. He usually tells me when he's going away for any length—"

"I don't know where he is," she says. "And don't act like him being gone is new. He's gone lots. You know where to call him. What do you need here?"

I agree with her and introduce myself. She says her name is Riley. She shakes my hand in a wary fashion. Her grip is firm.

For a woman her age her eyeliner is heavy—and mostly on her lower lids. I think of Lucinda Williams. "So you're Terrell's sister?" I ask, "He's mentioned your truck. We've never met but you called me a couple times mistakenly last year. My number was on the fridge when you were last out."

"Half-sister. I'm Terrell's half-sister. My mom married his dad. And those calls weren't mistakes." She takes a step towards me. "You know that from the house we can see you at the window, right?"

I hadn't realized my entire shuffling routine was backlit and visible.

I step back awkwardly, in pain, and begin laughing, and then Riley begins laughing. She hoists herself into the bed of her truck. She chucks a rolling suitcase out of the truck and lets it tumble wildly partway down the drive. She's standing in the back of the truck grinning. I chase the suitcase in my own personal hobbled way.

"You're the widower," Riley says from the truck. And I don't respond. I pull her suitcase up the drive. I'm breathing heavily.

"What happened to her, again?" Riley asks, as I hand over the luggage. I say nothing. I would never tell her what happened, even if it would be a familiar story, one she might have experienced in her own life. I would never tell her, but I will tell you.

o

She was driving home; Beth was driving home. She was supposed to meet the Umbers' at their restaurant, they were going to keep the blinds down and sit and have a glass of wine, everyone's workday done. Maybe play a little music and take turns dancing with Barnes. That was the plan. For Beth to have her glass of wine, take her time, maybe eat, and meet me at home. I had work to do and would be up when she got home. She didn't meet up with Lucia and Barnes though, she begged off, saying she wanted to have dinner with me at the house. There was an accident. No one was drunk. It wasn't an old man or old woman who shouldn't have been driving, who could barely see. It was kid in a pickup truck. A young kid out with his girlfriend. His head turned, talking to her, maybe staring at her, thinking of what the night might hold. Beth was at an intersection, a busy intersection waiting, and the kid and his girlfriend plowed into her from behind. Her car's back end collapsed. Beth's airbag went off, and in the chaos she hit the gas and went into oncoming traffic exiting the highway. Other people died too. That's what happened.

If someone asks in a way that I don't find cruel, I'll usually just say, "Cancer." This ends the conversation.

o

Riley says my name, apparently for a second time. "Do you want to come inside?" she asks. "If you can keep it to yourself. Terrell doesn't know I'm here."

"I've never been inside," I tell her.

"Has Terrell ever been in *your* house?"

No, he hasn't. I can't believe this had never occurred to me. He hasn't been in my house. I've probably never invited him.

"No, never been in my house," I say. "Will he be back soon?"

"Oh shut up," she says dismissively. "The internet tells me where he is," Riley says in a vampire voice. Then, plainly, "His whole speaking schedule is posted. Anyone can know where he is. Every convention, every appearance. He's in Milwaukee. Then two days free. Then the whole goddamn Eastern Seaboard. Boston, Dover, Atlantic City—"

o

The house is narrow hallways and large rooms, shadowy even when fully lit. None of the bulbs burn yellow; the whole place is blue, calm, dialed down. A controlled environment. The kitchen is small and slate. Fit for one man and no cooking. The ceilings are taller than mine, but, this is hard for me to understand because both our houses from the street look like fairly basic one-level homes. Terrell's, clearly, is not. It feels possible to turn a corner in this house and find a low-lit single bowling lane. Out back, there is a glowing rectangular pool. The backyard is cut into the hillside, clean pink rock surfaces, light nooks set in the cliff itself, cacti evenly spaced on a stone shelf spanning beyond the length of the pool, and the whole of it well-maintained. Like the wind doesn't blow in this yard. The black van cleaning ladies are multitalented, because I've seen no gardener. It is a house for monied LA, not for hiding north of Phoenix.

I say as much to Riley as I receive her casual walkthrough. "I've said to Terrell it's fit for a cold-blooded reptile," she says. This seems right.

We settle into the gray flat furniture in the living room, which is sunk several steps below the kitchen and rest of the house, and I understand that Riley is sizing me up. I ask her why she's here now, and she says, "I've made my money for the month and was looking for a drive. I'm here because I have a key. *You're* here because I have a key."

I resist asking what "made my money for the month" means, and how it is she made said money. I tell her that I am considering going to see her brother speak. She does not correct me and say half-brother. "I want to hear the Phoenix Lights talk," I tell her.

"Ten years too late," Riley says, puzzled. "Longer than that." She turns on the TV and *Help!* is on. George is instructing the lawn man, pointing where to cut the indoor grass; Paul's glowing white organ is rising from the floor. Riley watches and talks, looking at me occasionally, "He hasn't given that talk in forever. He gets in the door by saying he is Mr. Terrell Presley, Phoenix Lights, etc., etc. But he talks about all sorts of things. I heard him speak in Nashville and the title of the talk was 'Knowing When to Gather.' Mind if I smoke?"

I assume she means grass, and tell her no, not at all, go for it. Riley lights up a Winston. She reclines on the couch, sliding downward in her #2 Vols jersey. More of her stomach is exposed. Her body is acting like a tired child's slipping down a chair, acting separately from her wide-awake face. She goes on, "So anyway, this 'Gather' talk was all about encouraging people to share what they see in the world, that is, and this is important, if they had proof of what they'd seen, even in a small, familial way."

"I don't follow," I tell her. The addition of "small, familial way," confuses me.

She sits up and says, "Ok, like, let's say you and I are living in suburban Illinois. There are big trees and green lawns and long streets. Brick elementary schools, baseball fields, commuter trains, freight trains. We have a little house with a bird feeder outside the kitchen window. It's red. And I'm your dad in this scenario, you're my daughter. I get up early because I work shift-work, and I'm first shift. I stand in the kitchen drinking my coffee and looking out the window at the bird feeder in all seasons in the early, early predawn. For three days straight in June, I see a blue grosbeak, hear its morning warble, but so early. Too early. Sun's not up. You, my daughter, you're sleeping..."

Why had she chosen Illinois? Did she know where I was from? Why was she inventing a hypothetical situation to explain a talk she had heard in reality?

She continues, "But I have three days' evidence he'll show, this bird, and so on the fourth day I wake you up, gently, and set you on the counter sidesaddle so you can see, and we watch this radiant bird show up chirping. I decided to share with you what I saw. It's small and we're family, but I shared.

Or something like that. His version, Terrell's version of that story had climbers, men with big, rough hands. And he then started talking about how certain events, large events like the Lights, need to continually be talked about because they are that wondrous. But, I remember his summation was along the lines of: 'Start small.'"

I nod, more intent on hearing Terrell speak than I was previous, and with the feeling that Riley is usually alone. She asks, "What is it that you do?" And I tell her the basics of my day-to-day work-life, and that I work from home.

"I work in homes," she says. "Massage therapy. Fold-up table."

Because I have absorbed a version of my wife's consciousness I have a particular reaction to some women. A sort of double reaction. We were not religious and I remained, remain, godless after her death, but if there is a holy thought in my head, it is her presence with me as I putter around inside my days. I can think her thoughts most clearly when I am alone with a movie, book, or woman. Especially meeting a new woman. This rarely happens despite what I've told so far. Those were her chosen realms: art and women. And me.

Art in that she read constantly, mostly fiction, loved painting, movies. Her people were idiosyncratic and did what they did hard, and harder: Antonio López García, William Stafford, Elizabeth Bishop, William Maxwell, Joy Williams. She loved Hal Ashby and Bob Rafelson, Alice Neel. Patti Smith. I regret that she wasn't able to read *Just Kids*. My wife didn't like people who accepted inherited norms about what their lives would be, about what their professions could be. The nurses under her charge would tell you this. That she fought for them and their sanity. Anyway, I can feel her judgment coming on Riley's profession.

My own gut reaction is a dull sexual excitement that the woman across from me is a masseuse. I won't ask, but I wonder if she is capable of working the pain from my ass.

My wife would not object to the job itself; I remember her slack-jawed amazement matching my own as we walked out of a tiki beach hut massage during our lone trip to Hawaii. We emerged from the low hut onto a beach under a gray sky ready to storm, with brilliantly white cloud-wisps fading, both of us stumbling like idiots towards our hotel, the shoreline ahead already caught in the downpour. But she'd be harder on the accoutrements usually required to make the massage profession a reality. The soft-spiritual talk, candles, moaning music.

"New-agey stuff?" I ask Riley earnestly.

Riley shakes her head and lights another cigarette. "My policy is, no talking. I have a white noise track I put on. It's just rain and at the end before it loops you can hear a car coming down a wet road. And no candles. I bring a lamp with a fader."

I nod.

"You could use a massage," she adds. "You look goddamn rigid."

Again I nod, unsure if something is being offered. I change the subject. "I want to go see your brother talk. I'm going to. But I don't know how to go about doing it."

"Well stop whatever it is you're doing now. It makes you awful to look at."

I put my hands on my knees as if this will alter my facial expression.

She goes on. "Going to hear him talk is not serious. He's making it all up. What made him famous is something that happened to him. Like a ball that was handed to him. And he's run with it, sure. But don't give him too much credit."

Again I move my hands, now to my lap. She gives a tolerant look and continues: "Make a game of it. Give yourself a plan. Map out a route. Make yourself a budget. Convince me to come with you, really try and sell me on it. Take me with you, because I can help. I can help you remember nothing matters. Make it fun, for God's sake. I can help."

o

I walk back across the street in the warm middle of a starry night, grab the mail I forgot to pick up earlier. Another *New Yorker* to add to the pile, bills, a coupon mailer, and a sky-blue envelope marked in tight round cursive. The return address is in Charlotte. No name, but I know who it's from.

Charlotte is where Gary and Trish Lotti live. Gary was drafted by the Seattle SuperSonics in 1993 out of North Dakota State, but never played in an NBA game. He later tried selling insurance in Chicago, which is where we met. Trish worked under my wife at Rush downtown; my wife liked her because she took absolutely no shit from co-workers but was calm and unhurried, almost to a fault, with her patients. Gary, a seven-foot-tall black man, rarely appeared in charge when Trish was present. She ran their show. Gary tried insurance, he told me in a bar once while we waited for our wives, "because everyone asked me if I was going to start selling insurance once the Sonics dropped me. Power of suggestion." He confessed he didn't know what "selling insurance" really meant until he was hired. This admission made me love him. He didn't last long with Farmer's and so Gary and Trish, by then pregnant, moved to Charlotte to be close to Gary's sister and her family. All that's nearly twenty years past. Their oldest is in college, the two younger ones scrabbling somewhere in adolescence; Gary's coaching high school basketball and hoping to move up to college. The note is on letterhead that matches the envelope, in the same practiced cursive:

> *Stranger, the bugs are out. Gary is sitting on the couch next to me watching game film with the headphones I purchased for him. The hook up is wireless so he can get the TV audio without me having to hear the sneakers shrieking and whistles and hear the parents yelling at their kids to run. He actually pays a man to shoot this film. He's griped at the school to have a kid from A/V come out to the games and shoot video, but the school told Gary there is no A/V club...* (I skip ahead.) *Is work what it was? Slowing down? That's*

what your last one seemed to hint at. I like the image you gave me. Gripping your hands together in a ball, saying your circle was closing. That's dark, Russ! I like it! Vivid! (I skim further down.) *We don't know the new restaurants and we don't want to have to drive if we don't have to, but we will, and this I promise, we will pick you up from the airport if need be. You have the phone number and Gary's new cell. You have the address. I'm going to make this pointed here at the end: Come on out. Visit. Love Trish, Gary, and do you know the kid's names? xoxoxoxo*

I wonder what Trish and Gary would think of Riley. I wonder what I think of Riley. Would her presence be alarming? Her truck would be, her uniform, but these components of her don't travel. Right?

Look how porous I've become, letting any woman that comes along take me by the hand and lead me.

PART II

⑤

We have a tall albino waiter who is being reprimanded by a woman who seems to be the owner of the restaurant, Big River Diner. The waiter makes darting eye contact with me from across the room. He subtly half-raises his hand towards us several times to indicate "One minute." Both his hands are lightly bandaged around the knuckles, almost like the taping worn underneath boxing gloves, if done poorly. The owner keeps glancing around to determine how many people are witness to her hectoring. The reasons why she would dress down an employee in plain sight, reasons maybe unknown to her, are unnerving to the point of me losing my appetite. I imagine her parents were monsters. She wears large glasses and reminds me of Marge Schott. The restaurant is very loud. Oldies radio can be heard underneath the talk noise, *fool and his money, son–ny*, the eating noise, the scrape and pound and bell noise. Our guy is the only male server, and after the owner releases him back to work I watch him attempt to catch up on his tables, hustling. All his jaded co-servers act as his supervision when he walks near the kitchen or the counter. They see getting yelled at has weakened him. He's like the unfortunately large middle school boy who can't remember to box out, can't remember the plays, wears a t-shirt under his jersey to hide back acne, and only wants to drink soda in his dark bedroom and watch bright cartoons. This is a man, our waiter, who seems to be receiving a lot of feedback on his performance, getting batted around while he works, and I feel for him. He is wearing a starched white short-sleeve shirt and a red apron.

The restaurant is packed. Maroon seat cushions and dark wood, gold light fixtures, mirrors, three dishes of candies at the glass front counter, perms, squishy shoes squeaking, gum and plastic straws, the rattle of silverware dumped on tables, women concerned with comfort in their waistlines, in their backs, arches, home-life. Women with names for their vibrators, churchy women, women with and without escape plans. Men squandering their days off. This is a meeting place for the senior citizens in the town and for the younger families in booths looking around at what they'll age into. There are red suspenders and trucker hats, truckers, and keys on lanyards in basketball shorts. Everyone is tired, we are tired, and those who have been served are eating as if attempting to get quickly drunk on their food. We are in a town off the highway in southern Colorado. Out the windows is the blinding wash of the high plains. It feels too early for the restaurant to be this crowded.

"I wish our waiter wasn't the albino," I say, leaning across the table.

Riley gives me a look, wanting me to hear what it is I've just said. She's in a different jersey now, same number, same team, but white. The away jersey, appropriately.

I say, "No, I know, I know. It just charges everything. It puts a pressure on our interactions. Not that. Not because he's albino. Can't you see how they're riding him? The waitresses are all on him. Only man on the serving staff."

I stretch my aching hands on the table, my knuckles tender. I've been gripping the wheel too tightly. We drove through night into morning. Squinting into the highway darkness, alternating between blue-blocker glasses and no glasses to stay awake. I slip my shoes partway off under the table, as if attempting to tolerate plane travel. My sciatica is acting up, stinging then numb through my leg. I've had hours more to talk with Riley; I've seen her choose the jersey again as we set off, seen something of her suitcase's contents, and think I have some context for her decision making, outfit-wise. She might want the jersey to project: a woman younger than herself doing art installations in a mid-size city, like Cleveland, a little installation in the corner of the gallery, scattered clothing in a mock-teenage bedroom and one live snake let loose each night. A woman with an installation in a gallery in a mid-size city that still has a high tolerance for sanctioned graffiti. Medium-fish, medium-pond type posturing. You might imagine her apartment to hold a shrine to some lesser television personality on the mantle; someone no longer in the business, a piece of the local color on a long-running show. But she also knows Vols' history, at least a portion. Fulmer, Helton, Manning. She knows wins and losses. She knows yardage and myth. But these are numbers I don't know; she could be making them up.

"You've had a terrible start here," Riley says. "And he's not albino. His hair is white, that's all, his stubble. His skin is pink. Albinos don't have pink skin. No melanin. White skin. Chalk white."

When our server finally comes to the table he says, "Hello, my name is Paul. I'll be your waiter, you know that, I see your mugs are flipped, I'll be back with coffee, and really please do let me know if I can make your stay with us any better." He taps the pen he is holding on the table, a closing note to his nervous speech, and tucks it behind his ear. Through the gaps in his bandages I can see his hands are cut up, raw in places, like he's been working on a car with his eyes closed or punching someone. Someone who wasn't punching back. Someone who wasn't moving. A little girl in the booth behind Riley stands, faces us, and begins crying for a Dum-Dum. I think, Mystery Flavor. Paul scrunches his nose at the girl like a rabbit, but she doesn't notice.

"Paul," Riley says, demonstratively turning to him like a woman with a neck brace on, an affected motion that somehow implicates me as well. "What made you use the word 'stay?' Nothing wrong with it—"

"Riley—" I say, wanting her to leave Paul alone. Her jersey sleeves are rolled up. Eating noises surround us. The phrase "sleepy people eating their slop" comes into my head.

"It's fine," Paul says. "I was the overnight man at a hotel for three years and I used to say that to the guests, 'Do let me know if I can make your stay with us any better,' and on my first day here, first table, I rattled off the hotel line by mistake. That table gave me a forty percent tip. Like I was being welcoming for real, is I think why. I've just kept saying it. Routine for me now. Not superstition. I could choose to say something else." Paul's eyes lift, he scans the seating area beyond us. I follow his gaze. No one can seem to leave this restaurant easily. Lots of stopping to talk. Everyone's lingering, a lazy gathering mob in the high desert.

"Like what else could you say?" I ask, wanting to know his alternative greetings. I want to know what is in this boy's head.

"Like, like, I could say, 'Some restaurants in these parts claim best breakfast, best prices, but our only claim is that's not the best bullshit we've ever heard.' Or I could say very little and just focus on smiling. Be focused on refills and smiling. Quickness. Lightness. Attention. Smiling. Liquids."

I make a face at Paul and try to smile myself. I want to know what he has in his house. Apartment? Room? Is there music that opens this kid up? Is it all electronic looping noise? Is he revealed more fully in the clothes he wears outside of work? What makes him unguarded? Is this Paul unguarded in front of me, what we are witnessing right now? Hushed swearing and good-old-boying? Is he working towards something with these paychecks? A car? A new car? A vacation? Moving out of state? Moving north? You hope moving, you really do, no matter what your tolerance for small towns.

Riley repeats what Paul has said back to him in a deep twang, "That's not the best bullshit we've ever heard!" and slams the table with her hand. She's late with this and Paul and I share a look on her timing. Paul is trying to not smile. The little girl behind us reacts to all the noise by toppling over in a bubbling wail. She'd been standing witness this whole time and received no lollipop. Her ruddy parents apologize to us in earnest and we say, "No, our fault. Our fault." All three of us apologize.

Paul then has his own bout of strange timing and starts laughing at Riley's southern-man voice, mumbling an impression of her impression, and as he laughs I can see he has braces on his lower teeth. No way this kid has an apartment, or maybe he does, maybe the lower teeth straightening is a part of his ascension plan. Part of my discomfort with Paul: he's at least a head taller than any of his co-workers, and the only male, and yet is subservient to the most dead-eyed, broken of the waitresses. He looks like a goony English bass player without a band. Paul stands for criticism from all comers. His size, his scattered joking: I can see some of what's in there, and what's clear is that he's caged by choice.

Riley is less charmed than she was initially, but she's awed now, somehow. "You were the overnight man at a hotel, Paul? Pale and up late. Did people make vampire jokes?"

"Jesus," I say. You cannot expect this kind of talk from a woman in a football uniform, not this early in the morning in this place, understanding she's sober and we're in public, and members of no team. Not when the rest of her so obviously snaps and knows. Or at least seems to know. So many others wearing jerseys have their heads lolling, mouths agape. I see them right now eating pancakes. Scratch that, drinking syrup.

"I'd make the jokes first," he says. "So they wouldn't have time to get a shot in." He looks Riley dead in the eye and then looks back over his shoulder. He does not look at me.

"Can you tell us a vampire joke, Paul?" Riley asks.

I'm dumbfounded by this line of questioning. I want to get on the road again and grab food at a gas station a hundred miles away. Get out of here. Eat as we drive as punishment. No napkins. Greasy-faced penance. My wife had no tolerance for mistreatment of waiters, waitresses.

"Why doesn't anybody like vampires?" Paul asks, and when we don't quickly respond, he says, "This is the joke."

"Oh right. Why's that?" says Riley.

"We all have bat tempers. I'll be back with coffee."

One of the other servers, a rail-thin woman with nicotine-stained teeth and hair like a tall gray poodle, glides up to our table and asks us in a gravelly voice if we are doing fine. We nod at her. She asks, "Paul treating you OK?" We nod at her some more. She asks, "You treating Paul OK?"

I try and get Riley to tell me what she is attempting to do with Paul. I use his name like that on purpose, thinking it will guilt her, but she's way, way ahead of me in understanding the manipulation of men and responds "*Paul is fine*. He likes me and doesn't know what to do about it."

The only way it seems to me you can avoid Riley's derisiveness is to be chosen by her as off limits. I am off limits in a direct way, because it's my car, my gas money, my trip, but all her fucking with Paul is indirectly aimed at me. I'm the audience. I don't want to know what makes her turn on someone: maybe nothing, or a logic unknown even to her. My wife would not willingly spend a minute with Riley. I change the subject.

"Are all albinos of Nordic origin? No. Now I remember we had a black albino at our school growing up," I tell her. "And you know Yellowman?" *Nobody move, nobody get hurt. Nobody move, nobody get hurt*, I think.

Riley stares over my shoulder into the belly of the restaurant. I see her eyes tracking, releasing. When we reach the point in a conversation where she has ceased to lead, ceased to be the authority by her estimation, or at least completely in control, she loses interest.

I ask, "Has an essay been written on the appeal of Nordic travel? Nordic murder shows? Someone, an American I mean, must have tackled this. Someone deep into *Wallander*. It's probably been written about thirty-odd times, Nordic appeal. I've probably read half those articles. Half those headlines. And if you watch that first series it has color and silliness in a way that the Branagh doesn't. The Branagh is a

Nordic perversion. Completely ungrounded. You can't imagine those people throwing up or pissing on the toilet seat," I make a face thinking about Branagh pissing. "Some of the pull, that Nordic pull, is already there in other things we are starting to love, or have loved for a long time. I think it's there in the Premier League, I think it's there in this idea we have of Ireland, I think it's there even in the idea we have of Alaska or the American South. Most of us don't live in Alaska or the South but we could travel there and speak the language, we—"

Underneath my words Riley says "You must talk at the TV" before raising her voice and asking, "You mean 'we' like you and me?"

I say, "Americans. Americans, watching and reading. Americans easily swayed. Coastal or young Americans. Watching and reading Nordic crime TV and books. Taking Alaskan cruises. Watching Liverpool and Everton and Man United, traveling to the South for a weekend on the bayou, helping to restore the Gulf, buying Son House posters, mourning Sun Ra, still helping to restore the Gulf, getting tasteful tattoos displaying ancestral pride in coverable places, reading *Angela's Ashes* as if it was about their own mother, people born in Seattle claiming Ireland as home—I'm saying the pull is: there's no language barrier. And that these places are, in this false understanding, only different than the United States by degree."

"So what?" she says. She's drumming the table with her forefingers. I should tell her this misunderstanding is a wealthy white American misunderstanding, but I'm not sure of that, and don't.

She goes on, "So, what? You're saying we should be interested in people not appearing to be like us, but instead exactly like us?"

I make a face. "That's where you went with that? Ideally we would read about ourselves?" I don't know how she arrived at that concept. Either I'm not being clear or she's understanding less than I thought. I say, "Maybe the ideal is we would only read things, watch only things we didn't understand."

She says, "OK, but didn't you say these people *don't* understand these Nordic shows? Isn't that your whole point?"

I grimace and shift my numb ass. "Maybe the ideal is we would only watch or read things we *anticipated* would be unfamiliar. Or challenging. But, taking in a story about ourselves and taking in something unfamiliar or challenging are not mutually exclusive distinctions. I could show you a movie about your own life and it might seem foreign. And it might be very challenging. You could anticipate it to be—"

"No, I agree with that. I agree. Part of the problem is our inability to sit in not knowing," she says. "That's from the first massage class I ever took. The bald instructor repeated that phrase over and over to us, 'Sit in not knowing.' Totally bald guy. Big old drooping mustache."

It seems to me she's lost the thread. Or maybe I've lost the thread. Or maybe this is how she will regain control. "Sit in not knowing." I say. It seems like something she might end her massages by saying. I think about the words SELFISH MASSEUSE in pink arching letters on the back window of a blue 1987 Honda Accord. Lanny McDonald driving.

"Exist and be comfortable without understanding, in any given moment, yet still be present to that which we don't understand," she recites. I wonder if she listens to audiobooks. Are there audiobooks that provide masseuses with malleable nonsecular worldviews? Are there any books that don't?

Paul comes over and pats the table gently with his beat-up hands, tells us the food will be out momentarily, and asks if we'll need ketchup or Tabasco. The words are barely out before Riley waves him off playfully. I again see his bottom braces as he smiles.

I want to tell her that we all "sit in not knowing" always. But I think what Riley's recitation means, whether she knows it or not, is *consciously* sitting in unknowing, choosing to approach and embrace situations we anticipate we won't be able to comprehend, so instead I say, "Example," knowing she is comfortable building hypotheticals.

"Let's say Paul takes us back to his apartment because we tell him we are reporters doing a story on small-town waiters and we'd like to see how he lives."

I ask, "What?"

She plows on: "We give him some money for his time. We walk into his apartment and he has a three-TV setup: one TV is PlayStation, the next, Xbox One, the next, Sega Genesis. Paul asks us to sit on the futon, and we do, we flank him on his black futon. He turns on all three TVs, and begins a game on each one, pausing the game after a set amount of time, six minutes twenty seconds, and moves onto the next."

The look on my face says: what an absurdly specific hypothetical.

"He tells us this is how he relaxes, but later after we smoke weed with him out of a tall bong on his tiny deck, he admits that he'd never done the simultaneous gaming before and thought it might be something we found interesting and include in the final story. An event that would survive multiple edits," Riley says.

I pause. "That doesn't illustrate what you were talking about. Because while we are in Paul's apartment, we *do* comprehend what is happening in front of us. Moment to moment we comprehend Paul's actions: he is playing video games, he is smoking with us on his deck. We just don't understand, until he tells us, why it is that he is doing it. We *were* talking about art that is not easily or initially familiar. Art that we know we don't know. That is a different kind of unknowing to sit in, as you put it. Or a bigger not knowing. What you just described with Paul is not knowing *why*."

Riley scratches her forehead with her thumb. She reaches across the table and takes both my hands in her hands. She places my hands palms up on the table, looks me in the eye and says "Sit. In. Not. Knowing. Sit in not knowing. Sit in not knowing. Sit in not knowing."

I'm not sure if she's refuted what I said or not. I do like her stories. And about present, conscious unknowing, I think: to what end? To see things as they are? To see the everyday as it is rarely understood? Full of mystery, full of deceit, full of purpose and no purpose? Why pay attention in this way? The question arises: to see the world as it is, must we also admit to not know the world? And I think about the kind of lie we are telling in Riley's scenario. I ask, "Do we ever admit we are not reporters, and that there is no story?"

Riley is flagging down Paul and does not respond to my question. I like Riley's hypotheticals. She enters into these constructs so easily that my guess would be her real life does not challenge her wholly. I'm guessing nurses create these hypotheticals less readily, new mothers, people with real pressing needs banging into their real bodies. Or maybe these people enter other worlds *more* readily. Or it could be about being alone. Entering other worlds, created worlds, is a privilege reserved for the person able to be alone. Or perhaps to live in hypothetical or created spaces is always to the detriment of those who can't be in that space with you. It can be a defense mechanism. That I know. Playing the role of a hapless widower, even knowing others know you're playing a role, is a defense mechanism—because they allow you to act as you will. For Riley, the ability to think about what she is thinking about and argue for her point of view in the way she is, is a privilege of having made her money for the month. A privilege of not having a family. A privilege of being alone. Not that others leading different types of lives can't think and argue about the same subjects: anyone could. But these are ideas we drifted to—and that's the privilege, the drifting. We share this.

Riley gets Paul's attention and asks for more coffee. "No, we never tell Paul anything," she says as he stands above her. He tries to act like he hasn't heard her, but he clearly has, because there's the bottom braces again. Riley is enjoying watching him attempt to play dumb.

We have lots of road left. I feel like we've barely started. I'm not sure if I understood all of what Riley was talking about, every word, or none of it.

Our food comes. I eat eggs, scrambled, an entirely different meal than the eggs I prepare at home—for one, there is no cheese, and two, here in Colorado at this restaurant, there are home fries. Browned and oily with a wonderful crust, salted, peppered, buttery-soft in places. Riley eats a steak and eggs, rare. People are still milling around. At Umber's the diners are most often alone together or in quiet couples—I see none of that here. I feel more anonymous in this setting, which is nice.

"At some point soon we need to structure our approach to this convention," Riley says, eating lustily, like an English actress in a scene where she is home from boarding school for Christmas, haughtily chewing. "Because I can promise that you don't know what you're getting into." An English actress in an American football jersey. The second person I've recast as English this morning in obvious America. No one needs to remind Riley to "make a game of it," but I'll admit her drama is infectious.

Regarding the convention, I'd been imagining an auto show, replaced with stalls concerning telescopic technology, recording devices, easy to use 3-D rendering software for re-creation of UFO sightings, and portly men in glasses. I tell Riley as much, and she shakes her head no. Paul returns with a larger knife Riley requested when her plate was set down.

She points at me with the knife. "Think smaller and scarier," she says. "And these conventions are not about the future. That's an easy mistake to make. These conventions are about things that, allegedly, have already happened. This is all looking back."

I slowly twist in my seat, attempting to liven my left lower half. We've driven through the night to arrive here for breakfast, a decision that Riley insisted on, night driving, saying it was important to change our schedule because, "For new adventures you need new approaches." I'm now wondering if that is another of her masseuse mantras. I'm ready for the hotel and some rest.

I ask her how far we are from Charlotte; we are going there before making our way to Atlantic City to see Terrell speak, going there for a brief burst of the Lottis.

She checks her phone. "Over a day of drive time left," she says, refusing to give specifics.

⑥

The hotel room has twin beds and a white bathroom, packed gray carpet. Riley lies down as soon as we enter. There is a framed watercolor of a spindly blue mountain hung above the TV. Our small deck faces east, so there is no dark suggestion of mountains at our horizon. In the parking lot below, there's an Applebee's not yet open for the day. I imagine the empty Applebee's, sun invading where it can, smells like a puddle of light beer and wing sauce mixed by a bored child's hand. The child not looking at what his hand is doing, instead looking to upper corners. I'm here, me, Russ, I'm here, just tired, stay with me, I'm here. After our breakfast, Riley is ready to sleep. I lay down too, but not to sleep, not yet. I need to try to learn something about these conventions. And we are not racing headlong across this country. When we drive, when I drive, we won't dally, but our in-between times will be amorphous, unhurried. I know enough to know I know nothing, so who knows, maybe we'll be forced to hurry at some point. Maybe I'll be forced to hurry. But, if we can laze about—this is my plan.

Riley puts her back to me from her bed, on top of the covers, and goes about settling like an old cat. She's having trouble. I watch her body realize her pockets are full. With a backstroke reach over her shoulder, Riley places the following items on the nightstand between our two beds: set of keys, large foldable pocketknife, and a napkin on which Paul has written his address. We are expected later on at Paul's, after Paul gets off work, for drinks.

The invitation came as an apology for inventing the forty percent tip story he gave us. A manager, the smoky poodle woman, had overheard Paul and made him fess up. Told him to show some respect. It was unclear how she knew he was lying, how she'd even heard what Paul was saying to us. We hadn't noticed her listening. We didn't care about the lying, and after Paul's confession we had turned to see if we could find the woman to let her know we were thrilled with our service, and (though we wouldn't tell her this part) thrilled with being lied to. Paul said, "I was trying to manipulate the situation. Sure. You throw out forty and you hope for twenty-five. I was starting a negotiation with you that you didn't know you were participating in. It wasn't honest. But it was direct. I'm proud of its directness."

Direct is not the word I would have used. Possibly, "indirect."

Riley had told Paul not to underestimate what it was that we knew, and then came his invitation for drinks. I imagine he would have preferred to invite only Riley, and maybe he did, but as he asked he received cues that at least for now, we are a package deal. Until that moment it's possible he thought I was her father. Or who knows, maybe he's as curious about *us* as we are of him. Maybe he actually likes company. I raise my head from my pillow and again look over at her, already asleep, fully clothed above the sheets. She'd closed the curtains but asked that all the lights be left on, the TV too, and so I set it to a baseball game, the Rockies and the Dodgers in LA, and I open my computer on my belly.

I've always loved watching televised Dodger home games because of the zigzag roof at the top of the outfield bleachers at Dodger Stadium. And Scully, alone, talking out into the void. But I root against the Dodgers and their beautiful uniforms and their eight-billion-dollar TV deal. I'm thinking about reports that younger people don't watch baseball, and that the Premier League is increasingly popular. Maybe it's not that it is a game played by people we believe are similar to us, as Americans. The real appeal could be that the Premier League exists in its past and future simultaneously: the small, recently promoted, bottom-of-the-table clubs, the big corporate clubs, the older dated grounds, the battleship arenas. There is no parity, and this is familiar to Americans. Look at the Colorado Rockies/New York Yankees, the Jacksonville Jaguars/New England Patriots. I'm saying the real appeal is familiarity masked as foreignness. But basketball is a much better sport to cite if you want to talk about a lack of parity. There's that line about basketball being the perfect sport for modern times. There's a shot clock, the game is played indoors in air conditioning, etc. I look for this quote on my computer and find nothing. I check the baseball game. Who chose to make the number on the front of the Dodger home uniform red? Who is this genius? I hope he's living. We'd sit high in the America West Arena watching the Suns; Beth loved basketball. Her favorite player was Wayman

Tisdale—whose last year in Phoenix was our first. My wife loved that he retired and did something completely outside of basketball. We bought his records. She believed that Wayman's was a name that held promise. I'd yell, "Do what you can," to Wayman and my wife would scowl at me; she hated a condescending cheer. My personal nickname for Wayman had been "Taoman," which became "D-Man," which through shouting at games became "D." "D" is the most inconspicuous thing you can yell at a basketball game. I'm distracted by memories of spilled beer, hoarse throats, stale popcorn, following my wife up the steep arena stairs, gorillas. I try and focus on my computer.

The first thing you notice about these conventions is the cost. $30 or $40 for limited access. Hundreds of dollars for full admission is normal. "Full" admission meaning you get in to every speech, every ticketed cocktail hour, demonstration, movie screening—most of these conventions take place over an entire weekend. The conventions are three times more expensive to attend than I would have guessed, and leaner in their contents too. Because it appears there is less for sale than at a comic-con, it makes sense that the bulk of the cost to the attendee is placed up front. The focus of most of the UFO conventions' marketing appears to be on speakers. On the reputation and credentials of the speakers. And most of these speakers are not firsthand witnesses to UFO events, commonly known (as I learn from my other browser tab, the Wikipedia entry for "UFO convention") as contactees. No, most of the speakers are academics. Or "former" somethings. Former congressmen, former professors, former government operatives. Most of the speakers are not the people who have had contact themselves, but instead people who are studying the people who have had contact. Other types of speakers one finds recurring are hypnotherapists, actors, directors, investigative reporters, night-vision specialists. And then, relegated to the margins, contactees.

A level of remove from the actual event is tolerated by people paying to attend these conventions. This may seem obvious, because a convention is already operating at a remove. People are not paying hundreds of dollars for contact with aliens, but paying hundreds of dollars for contact with *people* who have allegedly had contact with aliens, but *really*, even more common is that people are paying hundreds of dollars to have contact with people who have had contact with people who allegedly have had contact with aliens.

That last group, the one twice removed from the thing itself, is the group that contains most of the top-billed speakers. The people closest to the aliens—the people who claim to have actually been abducted, or claim to have spoken to aliens—are not privileged on the convention websites. Contactees are sprinkled in, but like in so many fields, the doctors and professors and people with conventional markers of legitimacy are featured most prominently. Not the ones necessarily with the firsthand experience. Or, allegedly with the firsthand experience, in this case. These categories of speakers are not mutually exclusive. One dual category is the contactee who, post-contact, obtained a "relevant" academic degree, for instance, an M.A. in

Counseling from Southern New Hampshire. And I learn, or observe, that abductees are understood very differently than contactees. Abductees are a class even below contactees—a further complexity that at first I did not recognize. Terrell does not fit neatly into any of the groups I have mentioned.

Terrell isn't an academic or in the entertainment industry; he isn't a contactee; he isn't a hypnotherapist. He does live in Arizona, which maybe second to New Mexico, is the American UFO hub, and if any of Riley's description of his "Gather" talk is accurate, it seems he is not that interested in talking about the implications of alien visitors. I'd like to ask him if a blue grosbeak straying from expected feeding patterns could have inspired him in the same way to give talks. If the content of the Lights means anything at all.

I can't take in as much of this as I'd like. Investigation is leading to evidence of other investigations. A book keeps appearing in the online information: *When Prophecy Fails* by Leon Festinger. The book is from the late fifties, and is a work of social psychology that describes a UFO religious group (whatever that means) who believed the end of the world was imminent, and what happened to its members when the world did not, in fact, end. I pay one dollar and download the book. The opening is as follows:

> *A man with a conviction is a hard man to change. Tell him you disagree and he turns away. Show him facts or figures and he questions your sources. Appeal to logic and he fails to see your point.*

I don't know Terrell's conviction, or if he even has conviction. I alter the information to fit my situation.

> *A man ~~with a conviction is a hard man to change. Tell him you disagree and he turns away. Show him facts or figures and he questions your sources. Appeal to logic and he~~ fails to see your point.*

Paul's house is not what I imagined it would be, meaning it is not a lone farmhouse atop a rise with foothills crawling behind. There is no skinny horse or empty flagpole. No orange cat skulking. Paul lives in a modern sprawl neighborhood like you'd find in Colorado Springs, though we are hours south of there. Families, small dogs, grilling. It's the last of the day and golden. There are multiple pairings of adults in folding chairs monitoring their children's play in the new street and on squared lawns. Frisbees hanging in the air. We drive slowly, creeping along, smiling, nodding at the natives. Riley looks dazed, says she could have slept longer. We were in the car for less than five minutes before we arrived. By some quirk of undulation, we can see our beige hotel and the lit-up Applebee's from Paul's front door. We can't see Big River Diner, tucked by the highway, and I'm glad. It would be terrible if Paul was able to see work from his house. In the gaps not yet built on, there are slopes of burnt wheat-colored prairie, raw dirt, razed earth ready for further improbable construction spiraling outward from this centerless town. The question, "Sprawling from what?" occurs to me.

We knock and wait. There is a black boy rollerblading. I look for a set of black parents among those seated watching, and find them already waving. The mother is wearing a Minnesota Vikings jersey and bright lipstick. We wave. There are shirtless little white boys across the street throwing a tennis ball high onto their roof and catching the ball as it returns tripping off over the eaves. I would love to know if they have a name for this game. Paul stoops as he answers the door. His white hair is not a choice. I say this because whatever he's done bathing-wise since we last saw him has given his haircut a boyish soft quality he's done nothing to offset, revealing the cut itself to also not appear to be a choice, but probably a result of saying, "Shorter. Round in the back." What I had understood at the restaurant to be inscrutable decision making on his part, seems now more likely to be a product of anxiety. He is wearing the same clothes he was wearing at the restaurant, minus the apron, which is more off-putting than it should be. I withhold, barely, the suggestion that he change.

Riley says, "You don't put on a different shirt when you get home from work?"

Paul says, "I changed. I have lots of these," meaning white collared short-sleeve button-ups.

Riley smiles and says to me, "Give him the money." I try and make a Humphrey Bogart face for Riley to see, but without his hair, I can't say what I actually look like. Humph's hair made his faces more hopeful. I say, "The money?"

Paul says, "This is a stick up."

Riley says, "The money for the interview. Are you OK?"

I say "The money for the interview," and I take $40 out of my wallet in twenties and hand it to Paul. He takes the money and smiles oddly. If this is the game, I guess I'm playing. A strong hope enters my chest, a hope that neither saw the rest of the cash in my wallet. Then again, I chose this, didn't I?

"We're reporters for *American Highways*," Riley explains, reaching out and touching my arm as she speaks, an encouraging gesture.

"Yes. We're reporters for *American Highways*," I tell him, primed now. "I'm giving that to you because we want to ask some questions about what it is like to be a waiter in a small town. We're potentially doing a story on roadside diners, small town cafes, etc. You know the type of story. Every year it's minor league baseball or 8-man football in Wyoming or a horse farm in Idaho. You know, Americana. People eat this shit up."

Paul is giggling. I don't know if it's because of how transparently false my story is, or because his life has become the sort where strangers hand him money without reason. Paul's foyer has dingy carpeted stairs going up, no artwork, and down a blank little hall I can see through part of the kitchen to the yard.

He takes a deep breath to get control of the giggling. "Who's the photographer?" Paul asks in the direction of Riley.

"Me," she says. "But no SLR. Just my phone. That's part of the thrust of the piece. Encouraging documentation, encouraging photographs and storymaking to our readers. 'Even your waiter is worth your time!' Some of the pictures I take will be attributed to made-up readers, just to tell the real ones, 'You don't need a fancy camera. We know you have phones, we know you have internet access—so, you know, do it.'"

"Sounds dated," Paul says. He drops his head and whistles like you would for a dog; he looks around, but no dog comes. I look at Riley and she's watching Paul. He says "Can I get a free subscription?"

"Done," Riley tells him. "We already have 'Paul' and your address, so we just need a last name to submit."

"Warble," he says. "Paul Warble."

Paul's house tells me a lot, and almost instantly makes me unsure about what we've started. His side tables, lamps, couch, empty picture frames, coasters, chairs, all are red. And not the same shade, or in any unified style. Brick. Terra cotta. Cardinal. Scarlet. Magenta. Rust. Maroon. These are clearly separate purchases from separate stores where the aim in each was to find whatever stock they had in red. A man entering a store to hunt red. The color is being imposed into this house in a way the house doesn't seem to be taking too well. Paul's hands too, healing, are red. Healing in a way that suggests they were recently ripped pulpy. He had bandages over his knuckles at the restaurant, but no longer. The rest of the home's finishes are basic, cheap, white or wood, the kitchen floors a patterned laminate, the walls blank, the bathroom faucet handles knobby fake crystal, the kitchen sink deep and tinny. And then all this red grouped in the living room. Empty red picture frames hanging. There is a large dog cage that might fit a German shepherd next to the television, but there is no evidence of an animal.

"Where's the dog?" Riley asks.

Paul says, "This house came furnished. Someone else's stuff. Came just like this." He pauses. "I'll get drinks and we can talk." The house looks tailored for one person, by one person, one set of fears and idiosyncrasies, but Paul doesn't seem bothered by us being here. He is not acting like the one person responsible for this interior, but I'm having trouble imagining an alternative suspect. Paul's version of bachelorhood bears no resemblance to any I've seen.

I ask for gin and ice, Riley asks for a beer, and Paul shows us into his backyard as he gets the drinks. I'll nurse my gin, because this is not exactly socializing, and I don't feel wholly in on the joke. There are four low folding chairs, like you might bring to the beach, set facing outward over his back wood fence. The yard is maybe forty feet deep, half that wide. The downward gradient of the yard is so extreme that the top of the fence is below the elevation where we sit. The yard is well-kept grass, mower lines uniformly sectioning off the lawn in strips as it steeply slopes towards the back fence. If the fence wasn't there, I can't imagine a better sledding hill. Beyond the fence in the distance is more of the raw and razed land we'd seen on the drive over, some of the wild high golden prairie, a large high school with two mammoth sets of bleachers on either side of a football field, four tall banks of lights, and a huge parking lot. There is something immensely appealing about the goal ends of a football field being open. Like a valley repurposed. Or, purposed. Because what is the "purpose" of a valley? Enclosed stadiums hold less magic for me.

Paul comes out with our drinks. He says he's having what I'm having, and we all stand and clink glasses before sitting to look out over his fence. My glass has the old Broncos helmet on it, the kind of glass common at antique stores. Paul's has a Raiders helmet. Riley's has a dishwasher-worn image of Elvis in a white jump suit. I can smell someone grilling hamburgers several houses away, and it makes me ache for hamburgers. I wonder if Paul knows about Fred Biletnikoff's hands. We are getting a Colorado sunset. Pinks and oranges and gray-blues. Paul tells us he's lived in this part of the state his whole life and that kind of color, that extremity of color, is typical. I ask him "Did you go there?" nodding in the direction of the school.

"Wasn't built yet," he said. "That school is two years old. Haven't had a full four-year graduating class yet. The growth didn't come to the area like was expected so whole sections of that school sit empty. I think the number I've heard is twenty-five unused classrooms. The deepest pool in the state outside of the Olympic training facility in the Springs is in that high school right there."

"Why build a school that big to sit empty?"

"Deepest pool in the state," Riley says, lighting a cigarette. Paul watches her drop the pack at her feet, watches her exhaling. He scratches at his neck.

"We want to record, right?" Riley prods.

"Yeah," I say. "Do you mind if we record, Paul?"

"Is there a release to sign?"

"That's not how this works," Riley says.

Paul smiles nervously so I can see his bottom braces.

Riley says, "We want this to be informal, Paul. You invited us over, and we are going to just sit and talk, so, you know, if some of these questions are too personal, or you don't have a strong feeling, that's fine." Riley looked at me after she said "you don't have a strong feeling," and I looked back at her, to communicate, "I don't know what you're saying either."

Paul says, "Shoot."

Riley starts the recorder on her phone and sets it on her bare knee. "Do you believe in aliens?" Riley asks. I try giving her a Humph face again.

"I think that whatever's out there will be something we can't understand. Not bodies or big oval heads. I think it will be beyond our grasp. Like the color blue trying to become more blue." Paul is pointing at the sky, the now-purply color above the mountains.

"Where did you get that?" I ask him.

Paul shrugs. "Why did you ask about aliens?"

Riley says, "Usually the answer to that question gives us a sense of the person we are talking to. We can get a sense of education, religious beliefs, or not, capacity for hope, general fears, and so on. It's one of those J-school questions that has stuck with us."

I ask Riley, "What kind of understanding do you think we'd gain from a person who answered, 'I don't care about aliens'?"

She looks at me as if we have never met. As if whatever we are entering into in the present is not happening and we are strangers struggling to level. She grasps for the pack of Winstons at her feet and sets it upright. "I would say that kind of answer is evasive."

I ask Paul, "So let's say you have a tough day at work. When you come home and are trying to relax, what do you do?" I am trying to block out the hamburger smell by holding the gin up to my face and inhaling. It works. I keep the glass near my face. I put my left leg out straight and wince.

"This house is owned by my sister and her husband. I stay here and pay them rent. It came with the red room, a punching bag in the garage, no boxing gloves, a dog cage; it's fine for me. My brother-in-law makes pretty good money, especially for down here. They give me a family discount. So I have discretionary income. I don't spend a lot on food, I spend nothing on going out, there's no going out really, so the bulk of my monthly spending is on Netflix, and the like."

Riley says. "How much do spend getting your hair that white? Do you use bleach? How do you get it bright bright white?"

I can't tell if Riley is trying to provoke Paul to get a reaction or if she really believes his hair is self-doctored in some way. From where I'm sitting, it's just the kid's got white hair. I take a long drink and inhale through my nose the medicinal juniper aroma. Seems unlikely that a married couple decorated this house.

"I'm telling you how I relax," Paul says to me, "I'm answering your questions."

"Go on," I tell him.

"The TV told me because I gave *Fargo* a five-star rating I might enjoy *Shadows in Paradise*, the Kaurismäki movie, and I watched that and so now I watch that quite a bit. I watched his other ones on there. I like *Shadows in Paradise* best."

"Is Kaurismäki Japanese?" Riley asks, touching her phone on her knee, maybe to make sure it's still recording. I try to imagine what she could possibly do with Paul's answers.

"He's Finnish," Paul says. "Like Peter Forsberg."

"Forsberg's Swedish," I say, "So you relax by watching movies?"

"Only that one movie recently. I play it again and again like a song. I like to find one I can watch again and again."

"Why do you like it so much? Because you understand it? Because you don't understand it?" I ask.

He makes a face at my question. "I like it because it has music and no music. I think that's true; music and no music. Some movies you watch, they get the really awful dark stuff right, but there's no music. And that's a shame."

He doesn't say that he means "music" in opposition to brutal chaos, music as in something composed, with form—hopeful—no, he doesn't say any of that. These are my constructions. But I understand what he means exactly. "Why are you a waiter at that awful restaurant?" I ask.

Paul says, "No different than what I was just saying. No music. And then there is music. Right? Here we are. And speaking of that—"

Paul leaves the sliding glass door open and places a little speaker setup on the kitchen table inside. I don't know if he usually does this, but it's a truism that music played loudly from another room is wonderful. He asks me if I want to pick something, and so I get on his phone and put on a record I haven't heard in years, *Here Come the Warm Jets*, the opening track shooting out of the speakers into the backyard. I made sure to hit repeat on the first song, trying to exist in Paul's house in the way he does: my chief goal when deciding to play guest. It's an opener that washes over you and pulls you under. It's driving music, movie music. I think about how long Paul has known we aren't reporters. I want to ask him. If we are playing a game, I want him to be a part of it. Scratch that—I want him to be a part of it in a different way. I want him to be with us creating the game. We sit with the music. The song ends and begins again. Riley hands Paul her glass, says quietly she'd like a different one if he doesn't mind, and another beer. Paul gets up and walks into the kitchen.

I look at Riley and she seems to be elsewhere. She's staring at the empty school, smoking. She's stopped recording and placed the phone at her feet next to the cigarettes. It's possible that for Paul the music was a move away from wanting to be recorded. I ask Riley if she's OK. She says she's fine and asks if that was all the cash I had, the money I gave Paul. I tell her it was. She says she'd remind me in the morning to stop at the ATM. I turn and ask Paul as he stands in the kitchen opening cabinets, "When did you know we weren't reporters?"

"Oh," he says. "Right now. When you told me."

This is Sunday.

8

Monday.

We have a day to kill so Paul can arrange shift coverage. I am content to roam the hotel. Smell the chlorine on the ground floor. Take the stairs down to the lobby for coffee, a higher quality roast than is complimentary in the rooms. Nod at the counter boy in the transparent rimmed glasses. Watch the business travelers inexplicably staying in this hotel connecting to the Wi-Fi, needlessly in suits because it's been hours—I've refilled several times—and they've missed no meeting. (Maybe being seen makes them work more efficiently.) And I want to reduce my expectations for Terrell, for the convention, even further. Not reduce, but refine. Clarify.

A question has come to me overnight. What can honestly be said to a group of strangers that cannot be said to a (for lack of a better word) friend? (Or is "neighbor" a better word?)

Diffusion is part of the answer, part of the out I will give Terrell. There is unquestionably a difference between speaking directly to one person as opposed to a room holding an audience that doesn't know you. There is a diffusion of effect with an audience, though, it seems obvious to say, not necessarily a lessening of effect, and often an increase, because transference of energy can be generalized and amplified by both the speaker and the crowd. That is, if the one on stage is any good. And if the crowd is receptive. Everything depends on who is doing the talking and who is doing the listening. Who is giving and who is receiving. There are not absolutes in the way I want there to be. The question I should have asked is: What can Terrell honestly say to a group of strangers that he cannot tell me?

Spoken convictions may be tested most when delivered directly person to person. Known person to known person. This is my belief. All sorts of bullshit can enrapture stadiums of strangers, whole nations of strangers. Look at U2, or field hockey. So maybe that's my problem. I want what Terrell has been giving audiences for years to be delivered directly to me, and that is not what he does. Not for anyone. He can't give me what I want because I am not a crowd. Maybe because I am not a stranger to him. Maybe person to person what he is saying is no longer true. Lucia and Barnes went to hear him talk, but maybe without expectations. It's worth pointing out that the majority of the hundreds of thousands of other Phoenix residents with a newspaper-level familiarity with the Lights and Terrell probably do not retain any memory of the connection between Terrell and the Lights, and maybe didn't even a year after the event. Regardless, I was not really taking in information very well at the time: unemployed, worried about myself. Not a lot has changed. If there is a difference I can claim here in this lobby, while suited men type performatively, it's that I want to know my neighbor. I'll skip social media, I'll skip the last two decades or more of political quakes in our country, I'll skip the new Batman movies, but I do want to know some of these people around me. Whether or not they want to know me, I want to try.

I return to the room with another lobby coffee and Riley is watching TV. She is wearing a sleeveless denim dress that hits above her knee, and red earrings like button candy. Her body is flat on the mattress and her head is propped on three pillows at what looks like a neck-wrecking right angle. There is a kind of defensive "fuck you" inherent in her combined dress/bed-posture that makes me want to protect Riley. The droop of my wet face when I get out of the shower occurs to me. My wife would say of Riley, on the ride home, if there was one, "She knows what she's doing." The TV is talking quickly in a high register. There have been seven shootings on the I-10 in Phoenix since we departed two days ago. No one has been killed; there's just a girl with a cut ear from a shattered windshield. The coverage repeatedly uses the phrase "ARIZONA FREEWAY SHOOTINGS," and I wonder if the use of the word "freeway" has to do with an attempt to separate the shootings from reality. "Highway" seems to me to be the term more grounded in reality. "Freeway" is a song word, a literary word, a word that doesn't seem to actually refer to the roads we drive on. Freeway is for prison escapees, Mercury Cougars, shattered green beer bottles as big as your head, a rash of hitchhiker murders. Freeway is for camping on the berm, building a fire that climbs a roaring ten feet high.

Riley's head shifts and she gives herself a girlish triple chin as she watches the images of the traffic grouped in the center lanes, as if the road's middle is bulletproof. (Girlish how? Maybe in that she seems unaware of anyone watching, or the standard practice of holding ones' head in any particular way in the company of others.) With the dress, she wears a braided brown leather belt. Her hair is behind her flipped up on the pillows and she wears no makeup. I notice she has a tattoo, four Xs, at her ankle. XXXX. I've been in the room for less than ten seconds when Riley says "Stop staring."

The plan is to rest today and leave early in the morning with Paul. To pick him up at six. To make him a part of whatever this is.

o

Riley says, "I want to drive over to Paul's house and see if he really has a punching bag in his garage."

I say, "I don't." I should have said, "Don't."

Riley lifts herself on her elbows, "It's the only thing I can't verify from last night. It's the only thing that bothers me."

"You can't verify any of it. It's possible every word he's said is untrue. We only know he works as a waiter. We've seen it. And even that, who knows? We know he lives in that house in some capacity. He may have never even seen the movies he was telling us about. He may be repeating a story he heard someone tell him. He could be lying to us just like we were lying to him."

"But we told him we were lying," Riley says, "And I don't care about the little things. I'm bothered about his hands. Something *really* happened to his hands. He either was or was not punching a punching bag in his garage. And if he wasn't, what made his hands all beat and swollen? And how he dodged my hair question. That didn't bother me so much, but why did he dodge that? And we are about to be in a car with this man cross-country?"

I agree to let her take the car, but I am not sure what she is so worried about. Paul seemed willing to do as Riley wanted. He even seemed nervous around her. And why a dress today?

I want to call Barnes and ask him to tell me a story, tell me what he's been thinking about, tell me what he's been hearing. Once I asked him his favorite desserts while we watched an old tape he had of the Fog Bowl and he answered, "Wedding cake. Fortune cookies. Candy corn," without hesitation.

I miss him. I should call, but instead I lie down.

o

I wake up because the phone on the side table is ringing. I feel like a lukewarm wire has been pressed to my legs where my jeans have creased and imprinted into my skin. Because I'd been thinking of Barnes, I expect the caller to be Barnes.

"Front desk calling, sir." Waking in the middle of the day, waking into a seated position on a hotel bed to speak on the phone with a stranger: I'm like a drunk in the middle of a long mistake.

"Are you the one in the clear glasses?" I imagine the front desk boy curling his toes in his sneakers, thinking about what he will eat when he finally gets home. A microwaved quesadilla. I don't know why my imagination refuses to grant him cooking skills.

"See-through frames, yes," he says. "I have a message for a Mr. Russ Lanaker. This is who I am speaking with, correct?"

"Speaking."

"Mr. Lanaker, I have a message I have been instructed to deliver verbally—in person, face to face, was the request, and I have..."

I hang up and pull shoes on, jog down the stairs in my sleep-creased jeans, thinking about falling down the stairs, hitting my head, being found crumpled and bald and twenty pounds overweight. Eventually the coroner might have a brief thought about the man who died alone in a cement hotel stairway, and once she gets home she'll hug her husband from behind as he sits on the couch. A real hug that he will not recognize as unique, that will not cause him to pause the TV. I shake the thought away. I actually shake my head.

The desk boy looks frazzled as I come around the corner from the elevator shaking my head. He's had a frenzied half-minute waiting. That's the terror of hotels: there are people behind the calls for room service and shave kits, and if you stand around long enough, you'll learn their faces. The daylight's gone gray outside—I've been sleeping too long; my nap has eaten the sun. One of the suited businessmen is still in the lobby, eating a loosely-built roast beef sandwich while looking at his computer wide-eyed. I think of that hanging chad election picture and hate that it's in my memory.

"What is it?" I ask the boy. He's touching the fucking glasses. Behind him—he's got to be seventeen or eighteen at most— a door opens slightly and I see a woman with a crew cut and the build of a wrestling coach watching us. She is wearing the same outfit as the boy, a black vest over a collared gray chambray shirt. The boy asks for my ID and I say nothing. I just wait. He folds after a couple seconds and lets his hands rest on the counter before reaching under the desk and retrieving two sealed envelopes.

"I'll give you the verbal portion first, sir. I tried to write it down but she told me I had to memorize and recite." The crew cut closes the door loudly behind the boy; he turns towards the noise before looking me in the eye and saying: "No punching bag. I repeat, no punching bag. This is not a cry for help. But, can you believe it. No punching bag."

The boy hands me the two letters, and I consider tipping, realizing I have no reason to be anything but thankful for him. I ask if she said anything else, not for me, but if the woman mentioned anything else in passing. The boy says, "She kept telling me to loosen up. Not to take my job so seriously. That's how she said 'Bye,' she said, 'Loosen up!'" The boy makes a face like you might behind the back of your cruel older brother, at what I believe was his memory of Riley. She shook the poor kid.

"How long ago was she here?"

"I don't know." He's done too, already in his head eating the quesadilla in his bed; he's looking like he might cry behind those frames he'd saved up for.

o

I put both envelopes on the bed. Neither one is marked. I wonder if it matters which comes first. No punching bag means Paul was lying about the subject Riley was afraid he was lying about. I get that. But "This is not a cry for help" means she's safe, unless the message was delivered under duress. And "This is not a cry for help" sounds like a cry for help. The boy's descriptions of Riley's jibes made it seem she was herself not in danger. This is a game: that's clear, more than it was before Riley and I set off. And this is not something I'd considered until now, but I feel freer in my thoughts while not knowing what is happening and while alone. Part of the freedom is omitting a woman I am sometimes attracted to from the room, avoiding that intermittent guilt, and part of that freedom is that not knowing and being alone are what I'm used to.

I open the envelope on the left. A handwritten note, blockish forward-leaning letters, blue ink, taking up half an unlined sheet of paper:

List of artists who I am more interested in photographs of (PORTRAITS OF SAID ARTISTS) than the work itself (PAINTING, BOOK, MUSIC, MOVIE):

- Willem de Kooning

- Chet Baker

- Ann Margret

- Tuesday Weld

- Gary Cooper

The letter is signed *Paul Warble*. What the fuck kind of note is this? If this note is from a void, I hate it; I disagree with its existence in principle. It's mean-spirited. A dichotomy is being created needlessly, though I would not go so far as to say falsely. And the idea of this list, this opposition, gives those not willing to do the work (not work) of actually sitting with a painting/recording/movie a way to speak about that which they don't know. "No, I haven't seen *The Friends of Eddie Coyle*, but does a person really need to see a Robert Mitchum movie if they've seen the Avedon portrait?" I would guess this argument has been made. The argument is possible, but not valid.

If this note is *not* from a void, if this note is pointed—if Riley told Paul what I aim to do in detail, regarding her brother, hearing Terrell speak, then I'm not sure what to think. Is this note attempting to tell me that all my guesses, all the hypotheses and complaints that I've extrapolated from the surface (portrait?) understanding I have of Terrell should be enough? That I should stop there and realize what is most powerful about Terrell is what I don't know? What I've invented? That there are no answers? Is this line of thinking any less fatuous when applied to a real person as opposed to the idea of a celebrity? Is fame completely relative? My mother is as famous to me as Robert Mitchum. Both are dead. I've seen hundreds of pictures of both. And if Paul is intending to question my search, why?

Am I making all this up? I say aloud, "Am I making all this up?" Is this a note from Riley who knows it will put me in knots, and maybe give her, them, some time? To do what? She does know how easily I am stalled.

I call Barnes and he answers after plenty of ringing. "Let me run something by you," I tell him.

"Ready," he almost yells. He sounds like he's outside.

"I'm going to read you a list of artists who are potentially more interesting in photographs, photographs of themselves—"

"Portraits," Barnes says; he's breathing heavy. It almost sounds like he's chopping wood.

"What are you doing?"

"Throwing rocks over the wall in the backyard."

"OK, so portraits of the artists I'm going to name potentially are more interesting than their work."

"Why?" Barnes asks.

"Why what?"

"Never mind."

I read Barnes the names and he says, "No one who has seen Ann Margret *move* would make this..." Barnes goes on for a long time about the body paint scene in *The Swinger* and the black tights/green sweater dancing scene from the same movie. He is exasperated. He keeps using the phrase "anti-human, anti-love," and then brings up an allegedly well-known black-and-white screen test from 1961 in which a shimmying Ann Margret, accompanied by piano and a man in sunglasses playing guitar, sings "Bill Bailey," "Mack the Knife," and maybe others; Barnes can't remember, but he says, "Even this screen test shows that the moving, living, woman—even the screen test!—that she is more than a photograph, more interesting than a photograph of herself! *Carnal Knowledge!*" And as Barnes is talking, I'm thinking about Margret's small commanding voice, thinking about the examples he's given, and realizing I only know something akin to portraits of her—meaning I only know the blips of her raw sexuality in these movies (I don't know the screen test— Christ, Barnes, how do you?) and don't have an understanding of Ann Margret outside of a handful of moments. Is this different than any understanding I have of any other performer? Margret's performances are completely overshadowed, for me, by the physical fact of *her*. This is weakness on my part. I am not evolved enough to see beyond her high breasts, hips, tresses of red hair, to the performance itself, the character, the woman. But is the performance itself more than the components I am not able to see around? Do I *know* any artist beyond the snatches of his or her image or work that I can remember? The physical fact of Ann Margret I can't see around is precisely what she is selling. There are entire movies about her eyes. Entire movies about her breasts in a sweater. Her cleavage. I'm talking three separate movies here. I put Barnes on speaker and search for "Ann Margret Avedon" and the portrait is telling. The information Avedon gives me is the distilled version of what I already knew about Margret. She knows how to *be* sex. I can't know if she wants to be sex or not, but there is no arguing that she knows how. Maybe that's it. A person does what she knows how to do, and we can either recognize her for it, or not. Intent is where all of this gets impossible.

I know with certainty that repetition and accretion do not necessarily signal understanding in the consumption of art, or with people. The inverse is true as well.

I saw my wife nearly every day for twenty-three years—of course, through sheer repetition, I have a life of memories of her. I can hear how that previous sentence sounds. It sounds like I am letting you know I won't forget her, that I am in no danger of forgetting. I am forgetting her all the time. Even now, as I deliberately invoke her memory, it is still Ann Margret shimmying behind her in tights, fists balled as she dances, my wife rolling her eyes in my direction. But is the information I received of my living breathing speaking wife fundamentally different, more telling, more real, than the information I receive from Ann Margret dancing in tights? It's shameful to suggest. Much more shameful than some lark of a list designed to razz a sputtering widower. Barnes is yelling to Lucia, now stomping around the house, yelling to Lucia, "You've seen *Carnal Knowledge*?"

Barnes' yelling rights me. There's another envelope to open. And who knows what awful list it will hold, or where Riley is? I want to save the other envelope a few minutes longer, because this does feel very much a part of the game. And it might be less awful than I imagine. It might say, look in the closet, or look in the sink, or get the map from the wrestling coach woman. Who knows?

I've abstracted completely from the original problem but feel I can see a shape now. Feel I've come to this: there may not be a fundamental difference between the way one encounters a photograph of an artist and the work of said artist. And one of those two categories might be much more interesting than the other. But neither of those categories is anything like standing and breathing and sweating next to a human being walking and talking and eating at your side. There is no art to us as we stumble through our days, and thank God.

But what I might suggest is this: the memories can be the same. The echo from Mitchum saying "Count your fuckin' knuckles" in a movie from 1973 is as strong in my head as anything either of my brothers ever said to me. And the line from the movie has broken apart from its context and come to mean something in its isolation that has lasted to the present day for me: make sure you see what is there. But I can turn anything into second-guessing.

Barnes has grown bored of my distracted grandmotherly listening noises and obvious drifting. He asks me to read the list of names again. "What a white list," he says. I wonder if this is part of the joke, coming from Paul. Barnes and I say goodbye. Apart from any large truth, Barnes confirmed what I thought. It is ludicrous that anyone who had seen Ann Margret in a movie would include her in such a list as submitted by Paul Warble. Of de Kooning, I can't say. Portraits of him, the intense overalls shots, *are* spectacular. Or the denim shirts buttoned all the way up and the baggy khakis; he really owns that look. But I don't know his work. If there is a thought I have on the contents of the envelope itself, it is this: Paul has not seen an Ann Margret movie, and as for the rest listed I'd say, gun to my head, those are only names to him.

I open the second envelope. *Sorry about your car.*

⑨

I spend fifteen minutes slowly circling the cloudy hotel parking lot on foot, passing the Applebee's twice, making sure the car isn't in the lot, making sure this is not a prank I can solve. I stand bending my dead leg. I want to lie down. Riley is not answering the cell number I have for her, which I am calling for the first, second, seventh time ever, in distress. I pay the boy in the clear frames $20 to borrow his car, after showing him, zooming in, zooming in on the map on my phone I am only going to drive five minutes each way. I leave my license with him despite him asking me that I don't; "Please, don't," he says; we shake hands at this point, and he says his name is Parker. It seems he's been here forever; I ask him how much longer his shift is, and he frowns out a grin. I ask where the crew-cut lady went and he says, "Long lunch."

o

I peer in through the small windows on Paul's garage door: no punching bag, that's accurate. I ring the doorbell, pound on the door: nothing. I step into the street and look up at the house, as if this vantage point will somehow be more telling, and I learn nothing that I had not already known from my banging and squinting and ding-donging. The neighborhood appears to be mostly at work or daycare. Four houses down, an unsupervised boy is on a driveway, flat on his belly. He doesn't have shoes on. He begins rolling to his left towards a little front lawn. When he reaches the grass, he stands up and walks inside. I'd like to know what scenario of his creation required such movement. It's summer, but kids aren't in the street. Today is a gray day. I don't know if the weather has anything to do with the absence of kids outside, or if there is some nearby packed strip mall daycare. I step back onto the sidewalk and hope the house will give me something. Give me something. I feel I have two choices and I choose to take both of them.

I call the Alamosa Police, the closest department, and am asked for my license plate number, make and model, color: silver, 2010 Ford Taurus, XJJ-677. I'm asked for my driver's license number which I say I will call back with. Then, the last time I saw the car, and if I am sure it has not been towed? I say that I am sure, that I was parked in a hotel lot.

"Are you a guest at the hotel where you were parked?" the voice asks.

"I am. Listen, I know who took this car. Riley–her last name might be Presley. I don't know her last name. I'm going to call you back."

I call Terrell and he answers, "Russ."

"Your sister stole my car."

"Half-sister."

A beat.

"We, Riley and I, are traveling together, but she left me a note that said '*Sorry about your car*,' and I haven't seen her in six or seven hours. And I have reasons to believe she's with a waiter. In the stolen car."

"Can I ask what those reasons are?" Terrell says. "And why you're with her at all?"

"I have friends in Charlotte," I say. "And she was going to meet up with you in Atlantic City."

Terrell is silent for a few moments and I try and match him. He goes on, "You went on a road trip with my sister. I am trying to understand why you went on a road trip with my sister." He cuts off the word "sister" sharply. I feel like I have been caught jerking off by an uncle. I feel young. Terrell asks, "Did she explain to you why it is she has so much time on her hands?"

"She said she'd made her money for the month?"

Terrell laughs. "Meaning I pay for her. I pay for her in all ways. You get that she's not well?"

I don't know what to say to this. I hadn't considered there was anything *especially* off about Riley. Not any more so than myself.

Terrell goes on. "I have stories about her that you probably wouldn't quite believe."

"I don't believe the one I'm in right now."

I bring up my car again, and Terrell seems to accept that what I am saying, at least about Riley taking the car, is probably true. Terrell tells me her last name and almost apologizes for his sister, half-sister, in ways that are both touching and defensive, the last of which is: "She doesn't know what she's doing, and hasn't for longer than I want to think about." The second part of that sentence is unlike any Terrell has ever spoke to me, and I don't agree with him. Riley seems to know full well what she's doing. Before we hang up he says, "Tell you what. I'm going to pay for a rental for you. Keep heading east. Go to Charlotte and see those friends, and then why don't you come up to Atlantic City. I'm giving a talk, I'll get you in, we can golf on the coast—"

I accept all of it. I am not too prideful to be paid for. And I expect Terrell to hang up then, but he doesn't. He starts telling me about the first time he met Riley. Better memories, maybe, if only because of their distance.

"The first time I met Riley was at a restaurant in LA. I had finished graduate school and was in California for a contract job with a pharmaceutical company that ended up lasting less than a year. At the time, Riley and her mom were living with my dad in his apartment in San Francisco for the six months leading up to the wedding. It's strange to put it as I did, that I 'met' Riley before we were made family, but it's the case. She was long-necked and slouched at thirteen, and alone at the table when I arrived. The three of them—my dad, her mom, and Riley—had taken the slow Amtrak south, twelve hours, for the weekend. Riley was third wheel, unwillingly and consciously, on this trip like a trial honeymoon. I remember Riley was alone at the table when the hostess left me. She was slowly tearing a napkin down its center. I told her who I was, putting my hand to my chest, misguided earnestness, I can't believe I did that, and I remember asking where my dad and her mom were, and Riley shrugging. She wouldn't look me in the eye. There was a beat. I had no idea what to say to her. I'd not known many only children. Then, the first two things Riley said to me were, 'How many of you are there?' And I told her about my two older sisters, married, back east, and Riley said, 'How does it feel to be my brother?'"

"What did you say?"

"I didn't know what to say. I told her I didn't know yet," Terrell laughs.

Now I don't know what to say. I'll be having Applebee's for dinner and so I would like to think of something to say, or have Terrell start speaking again so I can put that meal off for as long as possible. I hear muffled talking on Terrell's end, like he's covered the phone with his hand. "Jordan wants to know if she can come with you to your friends' house in Charlotte."

"Jordan?" I say. Eyebrows. White sports bra. "Am I on speakerphone?"

"No, she's had her head next to mine for parts."

Hearing the name "Jordan" is jarring, and my memory is stalled on her in my kitchen. "Can she hear me right now?" I say. Terrell tells me no, that he'll cross the room. I tell him no, don't do that. I say, "Tell Jordan I know what the kid at the grocery store meant about Richard and Linda Thompson. He meant they are great when Linda Thompson is singing. When it's her song. That's when they're direct and beautiful."

Terrell sounds like he'd had the phone away from his ear and returning says, "She's got headphones in now. But, right, I'll mention it."

o

My beer options are not "limited" within a strict understanding of that word. The Applebee's beer menu is a laminated half-sheet that I have to flip over to read in its entirety. A few of the diners' faces in the Applebee's are ones I recognize from the hotel, including the roast beef sandwich/hanging-chad man. He is in basketball shorts and a gray crewneck sweatshirt that reads "Northwestern" in purple across the chest. It appears his work is done for the day—and in his defense, he did put in a lot of public suit time in the lobby. He is seated at the bar alone, head up, watching baseball on the TV above him. Diners are scattered around the restaurant. The restaurant is not very crowded with people, but very crowded with banners and knickknacks, photos of locals digitized into black and white. The restaurant seems to have purchased a set of generalized 50s ephemera at a Wal-Mart. James Dean, Marilyn Monroe, Elvis. Monochromatic clip-art nostalgia and red roses.

The baseball is the nationally televised Monday night game, a three-man booth this year: Dave O'Brien, Aaron Boone, Mark Mulder. Roast Beef's feet are bouncing on the railing, sandals clacking. He is watching an oddly buoyant Mariners squad methodically destroy the dead-eyed Padres, as if Cano's smile has lifted a whole roster into the realm of belief. Roast Beef is watching with an intensity appropriate for someone with money on the game, although this feels unlikely in his case. I hate year-round interleague play, though the extra wildcard spot for each league doesn't bother me. Maybe because of where my allegiances tend to be: with the teams abandoned, with the teams treated as part-time hobbies by malevolent owners, with the teams who are truly successful maybe only twice in a lifetime. Many fans of such teams have memories—isolated and blurred at the edges—of holding eye contact with a loved one across a packed watch party on some balmy fourth-floor apartment amongst the bandwagon, mouthing disbelief and love: "We won." These are not just movie moments. I know because I've lived them. Or, nearly. But they don't come, not at the heights I'm describing, to those unwilling to endure a lifetime of the opposite. To be clear: the suffering is not worth the reward— I realize that now. I'm talking about bad baseball. The broadcast is talking about interleague strangeness because the game is out of hand and the rest of the talking points have too recently been stated, "*So, that's right, as you were saying, seeing old teams in new places and vice versa. The only series yet to happen is Padres away at Toronto. And that should be coming in July 2016.*"

The waiter comes back over and asks if I've made a decision.

Underlined beers available on draft.

<u>Bud Light</u>

<u>Coors Light</u>

Corona Light

Heineken

Miller Lite

Sam Adams Seasonal

Blue Moon Belgian White

Budweiser

Corona Extra

<u>Fat Tire</u>

Michelob Ultra

Sam Adams Boston Lager

<u>Shock Top</u>

Ask your server for a complete list of beers on tap.

I wonder why both the words "draft" and "tap" are used on the menu instead of choosing one. I tell him I still need a minute.

Roast Beef has a glass of beer in front of him. Hard to say what kind. Not that I'd have any problem with any beer decision he could possibly make. Drink whatever you want, Roast Beef. I hope he feels my goodwill beaming his way from across the room. Goodwill raining horizontally into his heather-gray sweatshirt. A left-handed specialist comes in to the game with the last name of Cale. I search J.J. Cale and John Cale on my phone to determine which one is older. My eyes are tired and I put on my cheaters, hold the phone up like a grandma making sure it's her grandson and not her awful neighbor calling. J.J. is older by four years and couple months. J.J. is also dead—a loss I grieved. I'm so glad both Cales were alive at all. Thinking about Roast Beef, and the money he might have on the game, and the brilliant Cales, and the also physically brilliant redheaded scowling Cale on the mound now—this raises me, raises my spirits, and I wonder if somehow I too am a recipient of the wonder that Cano's smile can grant. Can such a thing travel through TV? Of course it can—have I forgotten Ann Margret?

I slide out from my booth and sit down next to Roast Beef. This is socializing, and I will set no cap on my intake.

"I know you. You were staring at me earlier," he says. "And I could feel your eyes on my back just now." He says all this without indictment.

"And now we're talking," I say. I can tell from the softening in his face after I speak that he is smarter than I understood. That the shorts and sandals and the intensity he is giving off watching this game in an Applebee's has nothing to do with a lack of intelligence.

We introduce ourselves and shake hands and I like this man so much more now that I am sitting beside him and not guessing at his back. I'm going to withhold his name. I like calling him Roast Beef. I ask him what he does for a living and he tells me I wouldn't believe him if he told me.

"Why's that?" I ask. "Not why wouldn't I believe you, but why are we so wary of one another. And I'm not even saying you, necessarily, though you are a little wary, clearly. But why are we all so wary? Tell me if you could. Try." I can hear myself talking and I'm embarrassed because it is my gregarious, many-beers-in voice. The kind of voice that is foolishly inclusive. The kind of voice that I always regret later on, that I can't remember the last time I slipped in to, the kind of voice that I hope was less noticeably confident than I imagine it to be. I continue in this voice regardless, and do finally order a beer, pointing at Roast Beef's glass to let the bartender standing directly across from us, attempting to tune us out, know what I'd like to have. The bartender seems to hate me and I don't blame him. I'm not able to give him what I'm giving Beef.

Beef says, "Wary. Yes. That is the word, right? It's like if I really say anything about myself you might then somehow have access to my credit card information—like you might be able to download the contents of my computer and my phone onto a hard drive and distribute all that I want hidden from the world to the world. Wary might not even be strong enough. The word might be 'afraid.'"

I nod, keep nodding. I wonder what it would do to this conversation if I told him my car was stolen by a woman I was not wary of, but should have been.

He says, "The secret, and it's not such a secret, and it's why I think we are all so defensive, is we are goddamn afraid that no one will care. Even when we are asked about ourselves, we want to withhold, because, what if my answer is not enough? What if my answer does not encourage you to ask me another question? What if my answer is so small, so stupid, so not worthy of remembering, that you forget you were even talking to me, like the creaking moments following an introduction to a stranger at a party? The mumbling and shuffling and petering out. The turn for a new drink!" His sandals are really going now. Cl-cl-cl-cl-ack-ack-ack-ack.

"Right," I say. "It's important to remember when someone asks us a question, and really wants an answer, without thoughts of personal gain, that there is love in that alone."

Beef makes a face. Using the word "love" has opened me up to Beef, and I can see him closing down. I want to point this out. I point it out.

I say, "Like right there. I said 'love,' and it was a risk. Because maybe you'll think I was hitting on you because I used a word like that. An older man approaching. Or that it's possible that I will. Like I'm gauging your reaction. That somehow by using the word 'love' I am trying to open up this conversation to its sexual possibilities. And I'm not—"

But I've lost Beef. This has been an overstep for him, the talk of love; I've misread him somehow. I assumed he was a liberal-minded accepter of all based on the college on his sweatshirt and the political reputation of the city that university is adjacent to. But this was possibly a mistake on my part. Beef drinks his drink and orders another and I realize it's not that I've lost him, it's just that this slight turning in the conversation is one that he is not quite willing to follow me on. The bartender ducks out from the bar and heads towards the bathroom in long strides. I hope he has pills in his pocket and that he uses them to get through this shift. I hope he is not drug-tested, I hope he is OK. Everywhere around me I see men alone, whether they are or not.

We watch the bartender shoot us a look as he goes into the bathroom. Beef tells me, "I spy on the company I work for. Think of a secret shopper, but I work for hotels, one of which is behind us as we speak."

I want to grab his arm and squeeze it as a thank you for continuing to talk. I hadn't lost him after all. I don't grab his arm, though. I drink my drink and think of making a Clint Eastwood face. I'm much older than Beef and this kind of face might have an effect on him, though because I have little hair and am not slim, but yes, aging, I think the face I am making more likely favors a middle-aged Peter Boyle. *The Friends of Eddie Coyle* era Peter Boyle. Coyle, Boyle, Cale, Cale, Cale.

"So wariness, what you're talking about, it all makes sense to me. But the people around me *should* be wary of me! I'm spying on them," says Beef. "I'm the justification for their fears. So even though their fears might not be real, I certainly am."

I don't follow all of this. I don't know if Beef employs high-minded constructions when talking about his work because it is insidious, or what. Beef has transposed the word "fear" with the word "wary," returned us to where we started, and claimed he was proof that wariness *is* justified in others. I agree with some of his thinking, but can't track it in its entirety. I say "Fear can be destructive" as a way of bringing us back into lockstep, and he nods in agreement. I ask him if he knows the John Cale record, *Fear*, and specifically the song "Ship of Fools."

Beef shakes his head. I ask him a few more questions, and he doesn't even know Cale's work with the Velvets. I feel badly for him. He wasn't a teenager with those records, poor fuck. The self-titled record...wait, Jesus, Cale isn't even on that record, but the self-titled record came out when I was nine, I had older brothers that knew the truth, and I had tapes and a Caprice and the south suburbs. I have the "Ship of Fools" melody running in my head, and I feel like despite this man's thinking that I can't follow, I've been luckier than him: knowing the songs I'm talking about, having them in my past and memory and present.

I want Beef to be comfortable and so I attempt to make a face that lets him know I am open. Open to his unwillingness to talk music. Since Beth died, I've found myself trying out faces, slipping into brief imitations that nobody else recognizes. Who I am now is not really me. Sometimes I am trying to remember who I was, or who I am expected to be, or trying to embody some idea of a widower—but alone, I don't feel like myself, even though alone is now my natural state. The face I am making is one I remember my grandpa, hard of hearing, make while listening. A happy cringe. A face that is letting Beef know I respect his boundaries and understand that our contact is potentially limited. So I ask him, "What is your stake in this game?"

"This ball game?" he asks. He waves his hand at the TV, meaning: none.

Now that I know again that I haven't lost him, that he's stayed with me, that I'm here and he's here, I say: "The thing I've been thinking is: maybe we are not more than what it is we are afraid of. Because think with me here: if you take away what you are afraid of, you are a person listening. There is no projection of fear. You are taking in the world. You are a person standing in his body, in the moment. Without fear, we become blank."

"How do the things we love factor in?" asks Beef.

He's used the word back at me, "love," and I know then that my imaginary fears about what he understood of my intentions, sexual or otherwise, were invented. Of his question, how do the things we love factor in to who it is that we are? My gut right now on this is that the things we love are no different than the things we are afraid of losing, but to say this out loud to Beef I feel would be hateful and not in the spirit of our connection, of Cano's smile, of the grace present in the hopefully sedated bartender allowing us room regardless of his reasons, of the chancy beauty here at an Applebee's in the parking lot of a chain hotel in southern Colorado, so, instead I give Beef not my gut but the true answer, "I don't know."

He asks me where I'm headed, and I am reminded that this is an answer I should have by now. Without a car in the immediate present, all previous destinations are now in question, so I answer with, "Not Charlotte and not Atlantic City." There is the rental offer from Terrell, one I will take him up on, but I don't know in what way.

Beef's job occurs to me. "Spying to what end?" I ask. He tells me his job is not simply to ensure compliance of company policy, though the position was saddled with such obligations in what he calls "the old days." He says he is tasked with identifying "rising talent" in the company, and making sure managers on a local level are supportive of their staffs, and cognizant of operational trouble spots. Beef goes on: "Staffing turnover at our hotels has slowed down, which is counterintuitive because the economy has rebounded a bit, but these younger folks nowadays are more security-minded than we were..." (His assertion that we are of the same generation bothers and joys me.) "...they want health insurance, they want a regular paycheck, they want safety." I have no idea if Beef is right, but I hope he is wrong.

I tell him what Parker Clear Frames did for me. I tell him of the loaner vehicle, the message delivery, the way the crew-cut leaves him stranded daily to deal with difficult guests, like myself. I tell him my entire hotel experience here outside of Alamosa would have been much worse had it not been for Parker Clear Frames. Beef nods seriously. He takes out his phone and I watch him type, "Parker, young, front desk, day-shift, glasses," into his notes. I say if that hotel has any rising talent, it's Parker Clear Frames.

The bartender is directly across from us and has been listening for an indeterminate amount of time. We both realize his reappearance after Beef puts his phone back in his pocket. I order more drinks. Gin and tonics. The bartender sets down our drinks at the same time, the glasses very close to one another, in a way that seems to suggest he suspects romantic love between Beef and me. He asks, "How did you two meet?"

I say "On-line" as if it is a hyphenated word, and reach to pat Beef's hand resting on the bar, hoping to expand the lie. Beef smiles at me, but sets his hands on his lap, rejecting the move with a laugh.

The bartender says, "One of the free sites."

o

I stare drunkenly at the painting of the spindly mountain and have the hotel TV on mute. A letter is unfair for Trish. I already called three (?) days ago to tell her I was coming with Riley, and she requested another call if anything changed.

She anticipated change. In the past ten years I've flaked twice on a visit, but never when so far along towards making Charlotte a reality. Since Beth died I've received emailed photographs of their children growing taller, pictures of Gary's Sonics tattoo he got following the team's departure for Oklahoma City, snapshots of the deer that eat up their garden annually. I've watched their backyard darken with green growth. I've received Christmas cards showing Trish growing fat and Gary getting tired-eyed and bulky. Their kids are beautiful. But I've known for nearly the whole ten years, known even when I called Trish a few days ago, that I will probably never see them again. I'll never visit. At some point you reach a foggy plateau where you realize a friend, friends, are lost to you. If there is fault in this particular instance, it falls solely on me. And the attempt from Trish means so much. It does. But not enough for me try harder. That's the truth. The most they could give me would be a break from myself. A vacation. And that's not enough.

I pull up Terrell's website, my computer on my belly as I lay on the bed. The cities ahead of him are as follows: Atlantic City, Davenport, Lincoln, then he's home. Nothing scheduled for several months, the cooler months in our corner of the world. I don't want to drive to any of these cities.

I call Trish, and I can tell as soon as I start in that she is embarrassed for me. Embarrassed about the fact that I felt this type of flaking could be done better over the phone than in a text, an email, some more indirect way. Embarrassed that I would call her after drinking. In those other forms, text or email, at least she could speculate about the truth of the matter, be given the opportunity to, again, give me some benefit of the doubt. I am robbing her of that chance. I sound silly, boyish, weak; maybe so much so that ten years of widower status has now been deemed still not long enough to fully recover in her mind: this is my hope. I imagine Trish shaking her head as I complain about leaving the house; I can feel her not believing my car has been stolen; I can see my wife standing next to her, shaking her head. Trish says goodbye by saying, "I'll tell Gary. He's gonna be sad," and she means it.

Grouping my calls, I dial the man who has subbed into my consulting role during my walkabout. He doesn't answer, so I leave a message, asking how everything is going and thanking him. He texts me back as I change the channel on the television: *Everything is good, thanks for the extra work. nice help this month. Baby napping.* I write: *Could you stand another month of being on call for my clients?* I see the icon that tells me he began typing instantly. He says, *100% YES.* I type, *Deal.*

I don't want to drive anywhere.

PART III

Terrell is driving. It's after sunset and we can see the shadowy low mountains all around us. We are headed to the 101, and then in to Phoenix. I've never been in a car with Terrell. The Saab is as I would have guessed: clean, worn, polished, maintained. The interior technology is charmingly obsolete. The thin digital numbers on the thumbnail sized clock above the tape deck are faint, pulsing, as if maintaining a constant presentation is too taxing.

I think about where Riley is. It's been three weeks and she hasn't surfaced. My car was found in South Dakota, repainted, with Iowa plates. The Taurus' V.I.N. number was checked against its license plate because a German shepherd was left in the backseat while the car was parked in a IHOP parking lot in Watertown. A concerned woman named Grace Wendell called in the dog problem, a problem I'd bet she understood as a man problem. And she was right. Not long after these events took place, I was asked sternly on the phone by a police officer from South Dakota if I knew "a Grace Wendell." I said, "Of course not," in a voice that sounded like I was lying. This was two days ago.

I'd never heard of Watertown, South Dakota. When Terrell and I looked at the map together on his computer standing in his kitchen the other night, I had the thought: They got to Canada. They got away. "Canada," Terrell said, in a defeated voice. We both know so little about escape that we had arrived at the thought together. Of course, it's possible Paul knows just as little about escape as we do, and we'll be able to infer more of his progress. Or that there is only one thing to know: choose a direction.

Over the past weeks we've made phone calls, tried to learn more about Paul, and ended up talking to his sister and brother-in-law, now living in Reno. They were horrified to learn he was still living at their house; they'd thought he left a month earlier. They'd given him an ultimatum: start paying rent, or leave. He never paid. They had no idea what I was talking about when I mentioned all the red in their house. The empty picture frames. We found out the details of Paul's slim criminal record. A fine for illegal fireworks in his late teens, a minor drug trafficking charge, and the registered ownership of four handguns. Terrell said, "Let's hope he is the man he has been."

"How so?" I asked.

"A man who's done nothing."

And not a man about to do something, I thought.

The discovery of my car had given us a boost. It had provided us a place to begin, Watertown, that wasn't totally our own creation. Now we've spent the past two days searching with new purpose from our desert homes. We are not yet desperate. We got hungry together and ordered pizza and ate together and watched baseball. We drank gin until we got sleepy. A missing person removes limits on my drinking. We fell asleep and woke up. We made plans to continue. Terrell told me of future trips. He told me of a growing indifference towards his sister. He corrected himself: "That's something people say, 'Growing indifferent,' but that's not true for me. I shouldn't have said 'growing.' I've been indifferent and have always operated counter to that because it's the right thing to do." He told me Jordan was going to be living with him at his home, for the winter. The Canadian connection did not seem to bother him. I thought, a country taketh, a country giveth. I started laughing to myself. And then Terrell said, "You need to get out more."

"You need to get out more," is why we are in this Saab heading towards Phoenix. I am wearing blue because I was told to wear blue. Terrell drives rigidly, not as I would have guessed. I don't believe his driving style is an indication that he is uncomfortable with what we are about to do. I watch the numbers on the clock flicker. I like the look of the seven, an upside down L. We are headed to a Days Inn near the airport for a speed dating for seniors event. I don't think of myself as a senior, but it's what I am. I've never participated in any matchmaking. Pre-registration was required, no money is exchanged at the door, removing transactional residue, and as a result of early payment Terrell had access to the information that there are thirteen other 55+ men currently en route to, or already at, the Days Inn. And fifteen women.

I have agreed to attend because Riley is missing, not because I know Terrell is trying to get me out of the house. I didn't say to Terrell, "I will do this because your half-sister is missing," but he knows that the only reason I agreeably said I would go with him is because his sister is missing. And because he also agreed to participate. He started that way, saying: "Before I ask, let me tell you I'll do it with you..." He said he'd done events like this before, which surprises me. He tells me, "Being uncomfortable in unfamiliar ways is important every so often." He went on to tell me he believed familiar discomfort to not actually be discomfort.

We are southeast of downtown, passing over and through Tempe. I think about where Riley is. A line of thinking returns to me from childhood. Prayer thinking, guilty thinking, list thinking. Please God, help all those who need help, especially those in need in this moment right now. Please God, help those who are afraid right now. Who are in danger right now, who are trapped right now. Please God, help people escape that can escape. I think about where Beth is. I think about Barnes. I wonder what Barnes is doing. I never think about Lucia. She's too assured to think about. I think about Jordan. I imagine her talking to a man. It's a weakness that I can't picture her except in relation to a man. I don't know what this says of me in a broader sense, other than general inability. I look at the sparkling midsize high-rises of Tempe, technology and insurance, and think about college. Think about blonde women and red cups and violence. I think about what would have happened if I had worn a red shirt. It does seem to matter. We take a long sloping exit down off the highway. Certain possibilities are unavailable to a red shirt. I think about where Riley is.

Riley comes awake leaning against a wall in the corner of a crowded convention hall. She knows she has been drugged, she feels hungover, and waking into a crowd is making her headache worse. She is wearing her own clothes but her shirt is backwards. She looks for Paul and doesn't see him. In her immediate view she can see the backs of booths and plastic storage tubs that the various vendors are using. She can see tall blue cloth temporary walls used to form stalls for the displays; she can see the bright convention center lights. She sees lots of white people, and those that aren't white appear to be Asians of different sorts. Indians, Chinese, Japanese, Koreans. There is music coming from all over, competing for her attention. In the booths closest to her, a remote-control airplane is on display. She approaches the booth. The airplane is long and snakelike with thin broad wings. Along the back blue-cloth wall of the booth is an exploded view of the plane. A man is talking about innovations made with this year's model, mostly related to altitude capabilities. Riley walks away from the booth. She passes booths with drones, remote control tanks, R/C forklifts, detailed tabletop models of big-box warehouse stores given invented names: it's endless. She reaches one of the entrances to the convention center, a clear exit was not obvious to her, and she fights against the tide of entrants to reach the sidewalk, the day outside. It's cold. Colder than she ever would have guessed. She looks around her at all the bald, excited men funneling towards the entrance. She thinks about all the spouses happily left to themselves, men and women with a day alone, with the house alone, with the car alone, with their reading alone, and smiles.

Or Riley sits in the passenger seat of the truck and tries to calm the dog that is on her lap. The dog is so large that her head rests on Paul's lap. Paul is staring straight ahead, not signaling lane changes.

Or Riley and Paul found work in Wyoming. She's helping out at an after-school program and he's working at a paper bag factory.

Or she's wide-awake on a Greyhound bus, seated halfway back with her head against the window. She raises her eyes above the seat in front of her and sees Paul seated directly behind the bus driver. She can see Paul is talking to the bus driver, but she does not know why. Possibly he is ingratiating himself so that a future hostile takeover of the bus will be easier. Or it could be that Paul truly does want to know where the driver's favorite bar in Vancouver is. "I want to be the only tourist," Paul says. She looks out at the trees. She looks out at the occasional blue-gray vistas. She looks at the map of Canada posted on the seat back in front of her and reads city names she's never encountered before in any context: Olalla, Cawston, Bridal Falls, Coquitlam, Burnaby. She wonders if she will end up in one of these places. She wonders if one of these new words will become a part of her life like the name of a quiet co-worker. She thinks about winters, real winters, and she gets excited.

Or the decision to leave was hers. All of this her choice, and the speculation is irrelevant.

Or she is dead. Dead in a way learned from television, learned from movies. Cut up and cast off to sea. Sawed into pieces and put in acid-proof containers and made liquid by chemicals. Or drugged and thrown into a dumpster. Or held captive. Worst of all, held captive. Not dead in the real way: gone.

I say "He did have a cage" out loud in the Saab, without meaning to. I realize what an awful sentence this would be to accidentally utter while speed dating. The three words "While Speed Dating" echo capitalized in my head. I wonder if I was in a red shirt if I would have said anything out loud about a cage. The pressure of the dating event has me granting powers to my clothes that are not real.

Terrell says, "Who had a cage?" and looks at me with a face that knows all that I have been thinking—the black heart of it—and knows exactly who I am talking about. I wonder how much of him helping me, if this is what that is, runs counter to his instincts.

I clear my throat and look to the road ahead as I think Terrell might in the same situation. He says, "What the fuck are you doing?"

o

Arriving too early is clearly an anxiety for many of the attendees. Dome lights are on in several cars in the Days Inn parking lot, and in the other darkened cars are the darkened silhouettes of groomed and showered elder singles. The entirety of my focus as we sit in our own parked car is that, in a little over an hour, we will be back in this car and headed home. It is an adaptation of the retail work mindset I employed in my twenties. Eight hours and home, you can do it.

A woman is in charge. We all have nametags. She is the youngest person in the room and could be a daughter to any one of us. She has a modest gray dress on, a red bracelet. When she speaks, she lisps slightly, and her confidence in spite of the lisp, her evenly dispersed eye contact and calm, is powerful. Her name is Breen. The women have all already been briefed by Breen and shown to their respective fifteen tables. Breen and the women seem to share amongst themselves a sparkly-eyed private amusement. I wonder if Breen pointed out something she typically sees in the men who come to the 55+ events. Maybe she said, "These are nice men, it's OK to be excited." There is a square wooden table for each woman. A lit tea candle in the middle of each. The manner of dress amongst the fifteen women seated in this large conference room varies widely. If there is a broad comment to make, it is: older means more sequins and shorter hair. There are two similar looking brown haired women with sharp jaw lines that appear to be near the low threshold of 55+. They know they are the top picks. This might be a detriment to their chances, though they don't seem to think so.

Breen asks the men to take a step closer. "This part is just for you. They don't need to hear." We all take a step closer. That step makes me feel teenaged. Terrell and I have decided to act alone. We felt that separate experiences, no in-game discussion, might make the event more charged later. Breen goes on, "Some of your faces are familiar, but many are not. Thank goodness! This means we are making pairs!"

A man with glasses and a turkey neck speaks up. "Not necessarily, it doesn't." He looks around for support but we all turn back to Breen.

Breen smiles at the man and continues, "So I apologize if some of this is a repeat." She holds up three fingers. "One: Don't ask *personal* questions. An example of a *personal* question: Where do you live? Where do you work? What is your last name? What kind of car do you drive? Now, here's example of questions we *love*: Do you have a dog? What kind of music do you like? Have you ever been in a helicopter?"

The man with the turkey neck scoffs. Breen looks at this man, who's easily a 65-year-old, and without looking at his nametag says, "Last chance, William." The man does not look around at any of us, though we all look at one another. I watch William clear his sagging throat.

"Rule Two," Breen says, "is let's not get in to *specifics* of religion. You all know that as a baseline, we are Christians here." I look over at Terrell who is smiling at me widely. I smile back and mouth, "Fuck you, you motherfucker, fuck you." I realize I am having fun and look back at Breen who is saying, "You know? We are similar enough to share a table on sure footing. Right?"

Some of the women at the tables behind Breen are now standing and talking in little groups. I feel good that these women can do this easily. I think about my wife in this setting, me dead, her at a table. She wouldn't be at a table. She'd have to be tricked or owe a favor to be here. Well, like me.

"Rule three: No pressure. Have fun. One hour and you are out of here, either way."

I say, "Exactly!" and start clapping. Everyone looks at me. Terrell starts clapping. All the men clap. We are handed unlined notecards with our names on them and the numbers 1-15 listed and boxes running alongside under the headings "Yes" and "No." We are allowed four "Yes" marks. I wonder why there is a limit. Maybe to prevent the loneliest of us to check "Yes" to all. Four minutes at fifteen tables.

I start at table three. Table three is named Robin. I'm guessing Robin is ten years older than me. She looks even older than that. 55+, to me, did not mean 65. It meant between 55 and 60; I know nothing.

Robin sighs a lot. She asks me if I've done this before, which, I realize, is the obvious first question if you can't ask more traditional meeting questions, the off-limits questions. I tell her, "Yes, this is my second time. First time in this state," which, as you know, is a lie.

She sighs in a way that manages not to communicate that she is bored, but instead that she is under some immense pressure. She says, "What other state?"

"Oregon."

She sits up in her chair. "I'm from Oregon," she says in a voice that makes me wonder how long ago she quit smoking.

It's my turn to speak and all of the questions I am forbidden from asking occur to me to ask. I ask, "Do you still work?" and regret it instantly, thinking this seems like a judgmental formulation regardless of her answer.

"I do. I do still work," she says, seeming to have to force herself not to elaborate so we can stay within bounds of the rules. She also seems to be gauging whether or not I want to break the rules of the questions, or whether I was implying that I wanted her to.

"I didn't mean to—shit. I didn't mean to get us close to things we aren't supposed to talk about." She reacts well to the swearing. As if instead of "shit" I'd said "You're the best woman here." I keep going, "Well, what do you do when you get home from work, Robin?"

She sighs, and I wonder if maybe that is just how she breathes. I can tell she's going to answer honestly. She knows she's going to answer honestly too; she exhales again. "Lately I've been trying to learn about France. I paid for a special set of TV channels, they are some of the French channels. I get

Parisian programming. Next best thing if you can't afford the plane ticket."

"Do you read the history?"

"God, no. I want to learn about now. Modern times. I like French TV, movies too, because a lot of the attitudes, a lot of the characters, I just don't understand why they are the way they are. The attitudes are amazing. Does that make sense?"

"It does," and it does. "I like that a lot," I tell her.

"What?" she asks.

"I've never thought about 'attitudes' in general in movies. It makes me hopeful that maybe I can think more like you someday. See what you see."

Maybe you can't tell, but I'm flirting with this sighing woman. This sighing woman that my wife would make fun of in a way that would make me so thankful for my wife and regret having to talk to any other women, ever. But, I'm here, flirting. Robin knows it too. She puts her knobby hands on the table. No rings, her nails strong, ridged, and unpainted.

"What do you mean be more like me?"

"Old, open," I say, hearing my mistake and seeing a change in her face. "Instead of old, closed, as I am now."

"I see," she says, checking the "No" box in plain sight.

(11)

In the car on the way home Terrell tells me he checked "Yes" on all fifteen boxes of the speed dating judgment sheet. I tell him I didn't even think to break the rules. He tells me, "I hate to say it, but you're really being such a jackass. That's exactly the type of weak system you should ignore for your advantage." I wonder what is implied by "type of weak system." I would like to know other weak systems, and know how Terrell has ignored them. What does it mean to ignore a system? Can Terrell really be said to have ignored the systems inherent in speed dating if he did so in a collared shirt, if he spoke politely, and feigned interest with fifteen different women? It seems that "ignoring" a system in a collared shirt is the jackass move. Who knows. But mostly it is his insult that resonates. The insult makes me joyous. Jackass.

"So much perfume in that room," I say. "I forgot about perfume."

"Warding off the smell of death," Terrell says. "Women live longer, so they die longer too. Perfume becomes important."

"Can I say I hope you get fifteen phone calls? I really do. I hope somehow you are forced into paying for fifteen dinners and having dry, dry, painful sex, with fifteen lily-scented women."

Terrell likes that one and says "dry, dry painful sex" a few times. He says, "If I get any calls from anyone that sounds older than me, my policy has always been to say 'Terrell's out of town.' Also, I have your number to relay."

We are nearly home, five minutes from home. Terrell says, "What was it you were really doing with my sister?"

"We were coming to hear you speak. I never knew you gave talks. Jordan told me. Then Lucia and Barnes told me. They thought I already knew. And I told all of them I didn't understand why you'd kept it from me. Why you hadn't just told me."

Terrell looks at me, maybe to gauge how it is I feel about what I am saying. I try and look sincere, attempt a Mark Ruffalo face. Not quite a near-crying face, but a face that is willing to cry and sustain eye contact. A face that is forcefully trying to care and has readied itself for the present moment.

"Kept it from you? It has nothing to do with you. You're my neighbor," Terrell says. This is true.

He says, "We never spoke personally. You know that? You never even used your wife's name with me, not once, out loud. If she came up somehow when we'd talk, you'd say 'My wife liked X,' or 'My wife has a brother who lives in X,' or 'X reminds me of my wife.' That's not how you talk to a person you want to talk with. You use names with people you want to talk with. It shows that you anticipate speaking to that person again, and maybe calling back that name in a future conversation. It's building language between two people that becomes how they communicate. If you'd have wanted me to know something about you, if you'd wanted me to be a part of helping you understand something, or think about something or get over something, or even just talk, I mean Jesus, you would have said 'Beth.' I had to ask Lucia and Barnes, this is years ago, I had to ask them once, what your wife's name was."

"Why did you want to know her name?" I ask. This question makes sense to me.

"Why did you want to come hear me talk?" Terrell asks.

I hadn't seen that my actions, or lack thereof, had the same weight as Terrell's. We didn't, we don't, know each other. And yet, he trusted me with his renters. So why...

"So why didn't you let me in your house?" I ask.

"It's not that I didn't let you in. And if you're going to phrase it that way: *you* didn't let *me* in. *You* had boundaries. Boundaries like not saying 'Beth' to me. Boundaries like just asking me questions and not speaking of yourself. Boundaries like trying to make me laugh all the time. Boundaries like pretending to be interested in golf so we'd have something to talk about—"

"I'm interested in golf," I say. This is not true, but I feel the need to take a stand regardless.

"Fine—but what I'm saying is that you had boundaries, and they were clear to me, whether or not they were clear to you, they certainly were clear to me. And remember—I've never been in *your* house."

"OK."

"So, I made my own boundaries. If the opportunity to know each other was not available to me, that's fine. That would be forefronted. We'd talk in the street. We'd discuss 'business,' in the sense that we had any 'business.' We'd bullshit and I'd let you pry for the surface details and small talk that you were able to wrap yourself in and speculate about. I'm only thinking this now. You didn't understand that you were the one who made our interactions the way they were?"

I didn't. I didn't understand that. I still don't. Some of what he's saying is right. But am I guilty here of not possessing the skills to effectively argue my side, or is he right in a more complete way? I say, "I'm not sure what I understood. I didn't see I was doing the limiting in the way we talked. It didn't occur to me that I didn't know you until I learned about you and the Lights, your talk."

"Talks," he says. We are home. Terrell pulls into his driveway. He says, "It's not one talk. It's not even ever 'a' talk. It's that I 'am' talking. I make the distinction because it's important to me to think about it that way."

He says, "Because if I had a set talk, if I made it a bear talk or a blue talk or a Germany talk or a grocery store talk, I feel like that would be me claiming that I had figured out what it was that I was saying."

"Why would you be giving a bear talk?"

"Maybe I weave in a story about a bear. I'm saying maybe I weave in a bear story into the UFO stuff."

"Why would you do that? Have you done that?"

"I could do that."

"You make shit up and keep getting invited back?"

"These conventions, they are weak systems. The threshold for relevance is low, especially when you have pictures. Or another way to think about it is: psychics are established in this country. Professional organizers. OK?"

"OK?"

"I'm using these two examples because they both have a single talent. And from the outside looking in, it's dumbfounding that either can make careers out of what he or she has made careers of. In the case of the psychic, it's tricking people in the way they want to be tricked. Pleasantly tricking them, or, tricking them in an upsetting way that is somehow believable to the people being tricked because they feel they deserve the punishment waiting for them in their future. Because there are people, lots of people, who believe there is 'punishment.'"

"I think I might be one of those people," I say.

"There you go," Terrell says, "And the professional organizer, well, it's there in the title. They organize junk. The existence of the job helps confirm the belief that such a job needs to exist. Anyone who has ever hired a professional organizer has his or her life incredibly fucked. That's fact."

I feel that Terrell is wrong here. I mean, couldn't there be all sorts of people who have accumulated crap and didn't necessarily have the skills to handle this crap once they realized it was a problem? Couldn't these people be good people? Maybe not. I feel that I am also one of these people, these crap collectors. My crap is doubt. My crap is the accretion of doubt I have piled in my head. Doubt of the meaning of my past. Doubt of my ability to understand that I don't understand. Doubt in my ability to focus.

Psychics, organizers, "OK," I say, "But I'm not following what this has to do with you. What does this have to do with your talks?"

"Because I have one thing: I took pictures of what is believed to be a UFO. I have good clear photos. I took them. I also bought my neighbors' pictures. I have all of this compiled into a direct, simple presentation. That presentation is the starting point to each of my talks. That is, following a slide I put up of Robert Adams' introduction to *What Can We Believe Where?* which reads, 'Theodore Roethke's notebook entry was the victory I wanted: "I see what I believe."' Then I show pictures of myself, personal pictures, from that time. Me in sunglasses on vacation in Acapulco in shorts. Me in my Saab, a different Saab. Me and Riley attempting to complete a jigsaw puzzle. I am drunk in the puzzle picture. It looks like I'm her failed uncle. Then I show pictures of the neighbors who were willing to sell me their Lights photos, pictures of the neighbors themselves. I asked for personal snapshots from everyone I purchased Lights pictures from.

"I have pictures of people cooking, hiking, I have pictures of Barnes and Lucia at the restaurant, I have a picture of Barnes laughing on a boat and Lucia rolling her eyes. Barnes at the griddle. All sorts of neighbor pictures. Populating my talks with routine faces. Then I show my UFO pictures. And then a picture of me from the same time period, in pants in Seattle, one they haven't seen yet. Standard travel photo. Then I show my neighbors' Lights pictures, and again show pictures of the neighbors. Trying to normalize the whole thing. Next I show slides with a single word written in the middle of the frame: Cook, Banker, Teacher, Contractor. I tell the audience these are the professions or former professions of the people who took these pictures. I am attempting to separate myself from their prejudices, even if they have not had the prejudices I am protecting against, or if they are a part of what discredits so much of what goes on in this field. The insular, speculative, incredulous, droning, secretive frenzy. 'This field,' meaning UFOs, a field that I do not consider my field. My field is slideshows. Oral history. Secular congregation. My goal is to only posit exactly what it is that I know for sure, and that is this: all of these completely normal people took pictures of this event. It happened. Beyond any shadow of a doubt, the Phoenix Lights happened. What I don't know is what the Lights were. And I don't think it matters—"

"You don't think it matters?" Although this echoes my own thoughts, I'm surprised to hear him say this.

"It matters because it happened. I am never going to know what the Lights were. Even if the source was military and the military takes ownership—even then—what does that explain?"

"It explains what they were," I say. "Right?"

"It doesn't matter what they were. The point is that it happened. And many, many, many people saw it. But this kind of event is what gets denied all the time, in a much smaller way. I want, this is my aim, I do have an aim, I want people to understand that the *why* is less important than recognizing the *what*. It's the only way we can fix anything. To see what is really in front of us, and tell others, bring them in to that reality."

"What reality?"

"The reality where they see what is in front of them," Terrell says.

If Terrell has a goal, other than "to posit what he knows for sure," because what the hell does that mean, his goal is to give more talks. I think about scale. That the reason he is allowed such wild misdirection in his speeches, or re-direction, is scale. There is room within the event itself for a contrary or complicating view, in a way there wouldn't be if the event had been smaller. But I wonder, I ask, "Why aren't your talks more direct?"

"Because no one would listen. The photographs and 'evidence,' in that I'm using personal snapshots as 'evidence,' all is laying groundwork for attempting to reframe the audience's understanding of what it is they already believe."

Still no cars have passed, and, probably none will all night. The stars are enormous above us. The moon is large and graying the desert for the scuttling of lizards and snakes and bunnies and cacti.

I say, "The content matters. The Lights themselves. It might not matter what it is that they were, but the size and grandeur and stillness and mystery, that all matters. You can't wage this shifty, false embrace again and again unless the event itself can buoy a lack of understanding and make it enough for these people."

"What do you mean?" Terrell asks.

"You can say whatever it is that you want, and speculate in your own way about meaning and importance, but the reality is that these believers have the event in the same way you do for whatever their personal reasons may be. They can listen to you and disagree, say that the content of the Lights *matters*, hold up their own photos and have evidence for their beliefs embedded in the shape of the aircraft, of the pattern of the lights, of the ship's positioning in the sky, of the way it made them feel that night when they were home, after dinner, having a drink in the backyard. They can say that and be right."

"I hope so," Terrell says. "And I hope they carry that acknowledgement throughout their days. Not only that the Lights really did happen and that they have the proof, no doubt, in whatever way they choose, but that everything else in their life is real too. That we must have a fervent belief in the existence of others."

I look down the moonlit road between our two houses, the stars.

Terrell says, "Do you know that Gertrude Stein line? The one that says paragraphs are emotional and sentences are not? That's how I like to think about the talks and listening. Paragraphs are emotional, sentences are not. And one difference between paragraphs and sentences is space. Gaps. Time."

I think, keep trying. I ask, "Do they listen?"

"They listen, but sometimes they don't realize they're listening."

"The one I had summarized for me was the 'Gather' talk. That was what Riley called it. Where the father, a shift worker, sees a rare bird two or three days in a row and based on that decides to wake up his daughter to see the bird—any of this sounding familiar?"

"No. But that's not a talk I gave. That's a talk Riley gave you," he says.

"That's a talk Riley gave me," I echo, and Terrell lets my words stand, giving me a chance to hear them. I ask why he never tried to purchase my pictures of the Lights, why he never knocked on my door.

He says, "Do you have any?"

I tell him I don't, and he doesn't say anything more. I appreciate him not rubbing it in.

Umber's, Thursday, eight a.m.

The TVs are blaring. At the end of the counter one screen is showing updates of the highway shootings, the PHOENIX FREEWAY SHOOTINGS, interviews with worried commuters as they stand in their driveways and in front of their office buildings. Intercut with the interviews are shots of stalled highway traffic/streaming highway traffic. I watch two consecutive interviewees shrug. The audio we are getting throughout the restaurant is forcefully propulsive jazz. I flag down Barnes, who is seating the shiny young crowd, and he tells me we are listening to McCoy Tyner's *Sahara* alternated with Michael Hurley's *Armchair Boogie.* Since we've been seated the Hurley hasn't started yet, and Terrell says, "Tyner's got long songs."

The alternation between two musicians on the stereo is designed to subliminally highlight the Hippie Thursday "Pick Two" menu, Barnes tells me. Choose a special Hippie Thursday main entree and a special Hippie Thursday side dish from the "Pick Two" menu and a bottomless cup of coffee is included.

Of the Tyner, Terrell says, "If someone was singing over this it would be unbearable."

The restaurant is full of youth. Earnest couples that have loving/degrading sex and then smile with their straight teeth at each other from close range. Standing waiting for a table, their tired and broke faces near the door, but they are here. Gay, straight, other, all here for the restaurant's off-programming. There are elder regulars present, apparently game for a weird Thursday; they act as if nothing has changed, act as if they are not capable of being surprised or pushed off their spot. I imagine not so much opinions from these regulars as much as concretely set responses. One man in flannel and shorts is loudly flapping a newspaper at his booth, conspicuously ignoring the boisterous scene.

My wife's teeth were crooked. Physically it was the piece of her that provided the most mystery when she met new people. She was clearly an educated woman, evident by the way she carried herself, and she had openly come from a solidly middle-class background without financial hardship where braces were on many of her friends' teeth. So the question became: Had her family resisted out of principle? Was this immigrant thinking at work? Had she resisted braces so strongly as a willful child that her parents agreed? If you'd have met her, my guess is you'd have had these thoughts. Maybe looked to my teeth, straight, thinking my teeth might give you some insight into her teeth. I'd have no answers. The fact is crooked teeth are endearing in a successful person, and can belie all sorts of hardship. The fact is crooked teeth look better. None of that here. Straight teeth and healthy eating. Lots and lots of trying.

Terrell is smiling at his menu. He says he smells vinegar. He looks up at the shooting coverage, which has in the last few seconds become wedding season coverage on the morning news. Models are wearing wedding dresses and not smiling. He says, "I fully expect the news to have an update on Riley. Or in the car on KJZZ. I fully expect that whatever turn she's taken, there will be some larger ramifications." The music has devolved into cards-in-spokes-rhythmic-plucking and people are looking upwards for the speakers as if finding them will somehow redirect the course of what they are hearing. "I expect to find out what's happened, where she's gone."

"That does happen," I say. "People having breakfast and learning about their loved ones via national news. Happens daily." I feel he must be avoiding what is most likely, most like life, that she is lost to him, to us. That is my experience. We've both been duped, no matter what's happened. People are not constant, people drop away, people are lost to us eventually, and what is persistent is internal. What persists is the question surrounding the person. The alternate realities. Coupling seems like a defense against the fact that so many others will be lost to us. Almost like an admission of: I know I will lose all of you, I will attempt to cling to one. The attempt is futile, of course, and our spouses, our friends become lost to us in a variety of ways, but the attempt feels important.

I say, "Riley might be fine. Seems as likely as anything."

Terrell looks at me—we understand one another. When we are saying words we don't believe, we understand we are, but know nothing. The lights flicker and Terrell doesn't seem to notice. He says, "I'm ready to order and I'm ready to eat," and though I know it won't happen in the way I'd like it to, I hope we can try this again. Try to eat together like friends. I hope we can keep trying until we don't have to anymore.

ACKNOWLEDGMENTS

Thank you to my parents and Jaimie. Thank you Drew Marquart, Maxx Loup, Andy Wagner, Slade Kaufman, Pat Krillic. Thank you Parker Nusbaum. Thank you Brad Watson. Thank you Lindsay Hunter, Gabe Habash, James Tadd Adcox, Bud Smith. Thank you Siurong and Greg Pece. Thank you Jerry Brennan. And thank you Brittany and Mo for making the brief mistake of moving to Arizona with me.

ABOUT THE BOOK

Aging widower Russ Lanaker knows he doesn't know his neighbors—but when he finds out one of them was a witness to, and career expert on, the strange UFO phenomenon known as the Phoenix Lights, he realizes that's a situation he'd like to change. What follows is an odyssey out of his air-conditioned comfort zone, through the sun-baked Arizona suburbs, and onto the franchise-lined (and not-so-great) American road.

In an existential style reminiscent of Don DeLillo, but with the humor and heart of a Coen Brothers film, Alex Higley takes us along as Russ strikes out in search of knowledge about an alien encounter, and perhaps something far more bizarre—genuine human connection.

ABOUT THE AUTHOR

Alex Higley is the author of one previous book, *Cardinal and Other Stories*. He lives in Evanston, Illinois with his wife and dog.

ABOUT TORTOISE BOOKS

Slow and steady wins in the end, even in publishing. Tortoise Books is dedicated to finding and promoting quality authors who haven't yet found a niche in the marketplace—writers producing memorable and engaging works that will stand the test of time. Learn more at www.tortoisebooks.com.